A flicker of motion caught Jessie's eyes...

She turned back to the window. The intruder was still standing between the bunkhouse and the corral. Jessie left her observation post and hurried down the stairs, judging that the time had come for a showdown. Making no effort to move silently, she stepped from her cover with her rifle at her hip, leveled at the intruder.

"Don't move!" she called quickly. "Keep your hands still and stand quietly!"

⊷ WESLEY ELLIS ⊷

LONE STAR

ON THE
TREASURE RIVER

A JOVE BOOK

LONE STAR ON THE TREASURE RIVER

A Jove Book/published by arrangement with
the author

PRINTING HISTORY
Jove edition/March 1985

ISBN: 0-515-08043-8

PRINTED IN THE UNITED STATES OF AMERICA

Chapter 1

"I've been smelling home in the air ever since we crossed the Pecos," Jessie Starbuck said, turning away from the coach window. "And the closer we get to the Circle Star, the better it gets."

Ki smiled, the corners of his uptilted eyelids doubling into folds. "You say that every time we come home after we've been East."

"Well, it's true," she replied. "I guess there's something about this West Texas air that you can't find anywhere else."

Jessie and Ki were the only passengers in the observation car; the first call for lunch had drawn the other passengers to the dining car. A long wail of the locomotive whistle reached their ears, the warm wind carrying the sound to them in the last coach of the Southern Pacific's westbound passenger train.

"And when I hear the engineer whistle for the spur stop, I know we're almost home," Jessie went on when the whistle died away. "Doesn't it make you feel good to know that?"

"Oh, I'm as anxious as you are to get off the train," Ki answered. "That little one-room depot at the siding will look good. I get to feeling fenced in when I spend too much time in Eastern cities, where those big brick and stone buildings make tunnels of the streets."

Another whistle blast, and the train began to lose speed.

1

As regular passengers, Jessie and Ki recognized the whistle's signal. It marked the final curve before the little accommodation depot at the Circle Star spur would come in sight. Jessie jumped from her seat and reached up to the luggage rack to get her portmanteau. Ki stood up to help her. They were still standing in the aisle when the engineer began applying the brakes and the train slowly squealed to a stop.

A scattering of shots burst out from the prairie beside the tracks. Jessie and Ki reacted by instinct, letting the suitcase fall and crouching between the seats. Then a hullaballo of yells arose outside, and Jessie raised her head to peer out a window.

"It's only Ed and the boys," she said. "A welcome-home greeting. But every time we win a fight with the cartel, I look for them to strike back, and for a minute I thought..." Her voice trailed into silence.

Ki nodded. "So did I."

Ed Wright, the Circle Star foreman, came into the coach, two of the ranch hands following him. He said, "It's good to see you back, Jessie. Thought you and Ki might need a little help with your suitcases."

"That was quite a welcome you gave us, Ed," Jessie said, smiling, shaking the extended hand of the foreman. "And since you've got the boys with you, we'll be glad for them to handle our luggage."

While the two ranch hands finished wrestling the suitcases from the luggage rack, Jessie and Ki started up the aisle with Wright. He told Jessie, "I got your wire just before we started from the ranch with the market herd. We'll be shipping the steers out when the cattle cars get here in the morning."

"I'm sorry I missed the roundup," Jessie said. "How did it go, Ed?"

"Easy, for a change. If anything in the cattle business is easy, these days. We'll be selling just over eight hundred head this year. Not as many as we'd figured before you left, but you said you wanted a bigger carryover."

"Yes. But we'll talk about that later," Jessie said as she looked at the cattle that were spread over the prairie just beyond the tracks. "You'll want to bunch the herd for the night, and I want to get on Sun and start for the ranch."

"Sun's all saddled up and waiting for you," Wright told her as she stepped from the coach and turned toward the corral. "I figured that after all that traveling around you and Ki did back in the East, you wouldn't feel like wasting any time getting back to the ranch, where you can stop and rest. I ain't so certain I'd like the kinda trip you've been on. Boston and Philadelphia and New York and Washington sure sounds to me like too many places for a body to visit all in one chunk."

"Well, distances back there aren't like what we're used to here in Texas," Jessie replied. "But we didn't have much time to sit still and rest. And that's what I intend to do when we get back to the Circle Star."

A loud neighing sounded from the corral that stood beside the spur tracks. Jessie ran ahead of Wright and Ki to the fence where Sun, her magnificent palomino stallion, was pushing his golden head over the top crosspole. He tossed his head as Jessie drew closer, his golden mane rippling and tossing glints of brightness caught from the shining orb that gave him his name. Jessie wrapped her arms around his head, and Sun pawed the ground as he felt her familiar touch. They stood quietly for a moment in silent communion, then Jessie released the big head and turned to Ki and Wright.

"We'll catch up on what's been happening at the ranch when you get back from delivering the market herd, Ed,"

3

she said. "I just want to get on Sun now and go home, and I'm sure Ki feels the same way."

"It'll be nice to stop for a while," Ki agreed.

"You go on, Jessie," Wright said. "I'll send your suitcases back in the chuckwagon. It'll be leaving in the morning right after breakfast."

"Good," Jessie replied. "And when you and the boys get back from market, we'll have a big feed and maybe a dance. But we can talk about all that later."

She led Sun to the corral gate. Ki opened it for her and went in to get his own horse, a rawboned roan that he rode more often than the two other horses he used. Swinging into their saddles, Jessie and Ki waved to Wright and nudged their mounts toward the well-beaten trail that led to the Circle Star.

Everywhere Jessie looked, she saw signs that the arid range country was making the short transition from spring to summer. As she and Ki let the horses set their own pace on the trail to the ranch house, the air was dry and warm on their faces. The landscape was still green in the hollows of the undulating terrain, but on the hillocks and ridges where the hard soil lay thin, the grass was shading into a lighter green and would soon turn yellow as the sun's increasingly relentless heat drained away its moisture.

From horizon to horizon there was nothing to be seen but an occasional scrub cedar hugging the ground, an isolated mesquite grove or two, and here and there a patch of dark, bare soil where the ranch hands had grubbed out a cactus patch. Later, when the cowhands returned from delivering the market herd, the cattle now grazing on the even drier southern range would be moved into the area Jessie and Ki were now crossing.

To those accustomed to a kinder land, where rivers ran and the soil held the moisture of heavy winter snows and

4

stayed green even at summer's peak, the land would have seemed desolate. To Jessie, as to her father before her, the West Texas rangeland was home.

For Jessie, the Circle Star was a place of mixed joy and sorrow, for it was here that her father had died under a hail of bullets from an ambush by minions of the international cartel, which Alex Starbuck had devoted much of his time to fighting.

A self-made man, starting a business career with a small shop in San Francisco dealing in Oriental imports, Alex Starbuck had expanded into general trade in the Orient, exporting American products to the huge Chinese-Japanese market and importing goods of Oriental manufacture to the United States. In a relatively short time, Alex had acquired a ship to carry his own cargoes, then, unable to find vessels that met his exact needs, he'd gone into shipbuilding, which had led to the acquisition of timberlands to provide the wooden hulls and decks, tall masts and sturdy spars. He'd built one vessel, then a second ship and a third, and others in quick succession, until he owned a profitable merchant fleet.

Branching out from ocean shipping, Alex's interest had expanded to railroads, then to the steel used in the fabrication of ships and locomotives and tracks. One interest had led to another. To finance his expanding factories and his transportation interests, Alex had been drawn to banking and later to brokerage, until his financial holdings were as substantial as his other ventures. At a relatively early age, Alex Starbuck had become one of the wealthiest men in America.

Chance, in the form of a mortgage forfeiture, had brought him the ownership of a huge tract of West Texas land, and on his first visit to inspect the new acquisition, Alex had been drawn to the peaceful isolation the area promised. He'd created the Circle Star Ranch on the still-untamed prairie, and after the untimely death of the beautiful wife he'd married late in life, he had come to value the isolation of the land. He'd made the Circle Star his real home, a place of refuge from the hustle and bustle of cities. Here, Jessie had grown to womanhood.

Ki's life had been of a very different sort. Born in Japan of the union of a Japanese noblewoman and an American ship's captain, Ki had been disowned and disinherited by his Japanese family because of his mixed parentage. As a child he had been forced to live on the streets, begging for morsels of food. Eventually he had been taken in by an aging samurai, a master of martial arts, the indomitable and austere Hirata. It was to this teacher that Ki owed much of his physical and spiritual life. It was to Alex Starbuck that he owed the rest of it.

He'd first heard of the powerful American when still a small child, from his father, who had known Alex and admired him. Thus it was that when old Hirata finally died, Ki, seeing that there was nothing further to hold him to his homeland, embarked for America to seek out his father's friend.

It was in San Francisco that Ki found Alex Starbuck, who, impressed with the young Japanese man's intelligence and fighting skill, hired him as his personal companion and bodyguard. It was a source of unquenchable pain to Ki that he had not been with Alex Starbuck when his enemies in the shadowy European cartel finally caught up with him.

From the moment of Alex's death, Ki blamed himself for having failed his friend and mentor. He dedicated his service to Jessie. With the skill that was part of his heritage, Ki trod the narrow line of being Jessie's companion, protector, and friend without interfering in her business decisions or stepping into her private life.

Jessie gave Ki a similar understanding. From him she had learned more than a little bit of the skills of unarmed combat, though she did not approach the complete skill that Ki had spent years in acquiring. Jessie had also learned from Ki the wisdom of silence and the art of accepting and returning friendship without romantic involvement. Together they made a formidable team, for Jessie had also been tutored by Alex before his death in the intricacies of his great financial empire, and how to manage it.

She had inherited more than the empire, however. By keeping alive Alex's efforts to stop the secret, insidious tentacles of the European cartel from strangling America, Jessie had become as much a target of its vengeance as Alex had been.

They'd ridden almost halfway to the ranch house before either of them spoke. Sun was restive after the long period he'd spent in the corral during Jessie's absence. The big stallion needed to run, and Jessie indulged him, taking as much pleasure from his brief gallops as he did. The warm wind streaming past her face, blowing through her long, copper-blond hair, was also blowing from Jessie's awareness the muggy atmosphere of the East, with its constant dribble of coal-soot and industrial smells.

By the time the ranch house and its surrounding cluster of buildings came in sight, Jessie felt more relaxed than she had for weeks. She said to Ki, "Let's not bother whoever's filling in for Gimpy in the kitchen, Ki. I've eaten enough rich, over-seasoned hotel food to last me for a while. Suppose I just cook something simple for supper, and we'll eat at the main house."

"That'll suit me fine," Ki replied. "If you want me to help you in the kitchen—"

Jessie shook her head. "No. I want to do it myself, all the way from making a fire in the range to brewing the

7

coffee for after dinner. I don't know what I'll cook yet, but I know Gimpy will have some kind of supplies on hand that I can use."

"Remember, if you want me to help—"

"No, Ki. I have a feeling you'll want to be looking over the corrals and talking to the men who didn't go with the market herd, getting caught up on what's happened while we've been gone."

"If what the men in the bunkhouse tell me is true, things went very well without us here," Ki said, as he and Jessie sat sipping their coffee after dinner. As they often did when alone in the rambling ranch house, they'd eaten in the kitchen rather than taking the trouble to set a more formal table in the dining room.

"That's nice to know," Jessie told him. "But I'm sure that when Ed gets back he'll have a few things to tell us that the hands missed."

"Nothing important, though. If anything very much out of the ordinary had happened, I'd have heard about it. It's been very quiet, just as it is now. In fact, it's so quiet that I'm suddenly getting sleepy. Leave the supper dishes, Jessie. I'll take care of them in the morning. Right now I'm going upstairs to catch up on my sleep."

"I might just do that, Ki," she replied. "I want to fill in a few gaps in my journal before I go to bed. But I'm beginning to feel relaxed too, so I don't think I'll stay up very long."

After Ki left, Jessie glanced around the kitchen, decided to take Ki's offer, and went through the dining room and living room into the study that had been her father's. As she almost always did when alone at night in the familiar room, Jessie felt Alex's presence very close to her.

She took pen and ink and a tablet from the drawer of the

big, scarred, oak rolltop desk that Alex had used from the beginning of his business career, when he started his small import store in San Francisco. Then she moved to the leather easy chair that had also been his favorite. She could still catch an occasional, ghostly hint of her father's favorite cherry-scented pipe tobacco as she snuggled down in the chair's comforting depths.

Opening the inkwell, she dipped the pen and propped the tablet on her lap. She started to write, then hesitated, trying to decide whether to begin with notes of the conversations she'd had with the important industrial and financial figures who had been friends or business associates of Alex's, or to start by making notes of the political observations and forecasts that had been made by the President during her dinner at the White House and later, at the reception that had followed the dinner.

Then Jessie recalled the way in which the night had ended, and laid her pen aside. She leaned back against the smooth, soft leather and closed her eyes, remembering the rugged features of Hayes's young military aide, Major Jerome Carruthers, who'd been her dinner partner and had stood beside her during the reception. Unlike some of the so-called "family" dinners Jessie had attended in the Executive Mansion, this one was truly a family affair, there'd been no other guests except Major Carruthers, who was filling the seat Ki had declined to occupy.

Jessie smiled as the memory of her introduction to the young officer came back to her. The major's mouth had gone slack and his eyes had grown wide in the few moments between the time Hayes had said her name and the time the major had taken her hand and made a half-bow over it. His face was carefully expressionless when he raised his head, but Jessie had noted his earlier surprise and smiled inwardly, guessing its cause.

Later, during a lull in the conversation at dinner, when Mrs. Hayes had held her husband's attention with a long dissertation about the reception that was to follow the meal, Jessie had told the young officer, "I'm glad you've recovered from your surprise when we were introduced, Major Carruthers. I gather that I wasn't quite the kind of person you expected to meet."

"If I've offended you, ma'am, I apologize most sincerely," Carruthers said. "But if you want the truth, the surprise was a very pleasant one."

"I've always found the truth to be helpful," Jessie replied. "Suppose you tell me what you'd thought I'd be like."

"Well . . ." For a moment the young major hesitated, then he said, "When the President told me I was going to escort one of the most important women in the Western United States, I had an idea you'd be much older, for one thing."

"More like your mother than a—well, a sister, let's say?"

"Frankly, more like Hetty Green, whom I escorted a few weeks ago to a dinner and reception similar to this one," Carruthers said, a smile crinkling his lips below his neatly trimmed black mustache.

"Not the Witch of Wall Street!" Jessie said with a small grimace.

"Yes indeed," Carruthers answered. "She showed up in a musty black sateen dress that was beginning to turn green, carrying a huge black purse that she clung to all evening, even though I offered to hold it for her while she stood in the receiving line shaking hands."

"I've never met Miss Green, but from what I've heard about her fondness for cash, the purse was probably crammed full of money," Jessie smiled.

"Anyhow, I'm glad I was surprised," Carruthers said.

"Thank you, Major," Jessie replied.

"I'm really serious, you know, Miss Starbuck. I'm not

just passing on empty compliments."

"Why, I wouldn't think of questioning your sincerity."

"Now you're making me sound like a fool," Carruthers said.

"That wasn't my intention," Jessie told him quickly. "And I didn't classify your compliments as empty."

"Well, that makes me feel some better," the major told her. "I really do think—"

Whatever the young officer was going to say was lost when the President and his wife ended their discussion. Hayes looked across the table at Jessie and said, "It's about time for us to go into the reception room, Miss Starbuck. If you and Major Carruthers have finished..."

"Of course," Jessie replied. Carruthers leaped up and pulled her chair away as Jessie rose; then, as the President offered her his arm, the young officer stepped back to escort Mrs. Hayes.

To Jessie's relief, the reception room was not filled with an indiscriminate group of people. When she saw the guests and recognized a number of them, Jessie realized at once that, like the skilled politician he was, President Hayes had limited the invitation list to people in whom Jessie might be interested from the standpoint of the varied Starbuck enterprises. There was the Attorney General, the secretaries of the Treasury and Agriculture, and a scattering of congressmen from states in which the Starbuck interests were prominently represented.

With such a group, the reception line moved smoothly until a senator notorious for his verbosity stopped to talk to President Hayes. When Carruthers saw that Jessie was standing alone, her attention unoccupied, he stepped up beside her to bridge the awkward gap.

"Thank you, Major," Jessie whispered. "It's thoughtful of you to keep me from looking a bit foolish."

"Don't thank me before you realize that I'm being selfish as well as considerate," Carruthers told her in an equally low voice. "I didn't get a chance to finish what I started to say when the President ended our dinner. I was about to tell you that I think you're one of the most fascinating women I've ever met, and in view of the notoriously skimpy meals Mrs. Hayes serves, I was also intending to ask you to have a bite of supper with me after the reception."

Somewhat to her own surprise, Jessie heard herself saying, "That's very thoughtful of you, Major. By the time this is over with, I'm sure I'll be hungry enough to enjoy it."

Chapter 2

During the next hour or more, between chats with the guests at the reception, Jessie had watched young Major Carruthers and liked the manner in which he'd acted, a manner that gave no hint of the unspoken implications of the late supper they would be sharing. When he went about his duties in what she was sure was a normal manner, giving her only the formal attention that was called for by their positions and the occasion, she relaxed.

As the guests trickled away, Jessie noticed increasing signs that Mrs. Hayes wanted to bring the evening to an end. At last the First Lady's patience ended. She took the President by the arm and almost lifted him from his chair. Hayes followed his wife's example by bowing to the guests, then took her arm and together they walked slowly out of the ballroom.

Their departure started a general move toward the exit doors. Jessie saw Major Carruthers coming toward her, carrying the shawl she'd brought instead of a coat. The young officer smiled as he helped her arrange the light woolen knitted shawl over her shoulders and said, "I hope all the folderol hasn't tired you too much to enjoy our supper, Miss Starbuck."

"It hasn't. And since we're going to be out of the public

eye now, I think it's time for you to start calling me Jessie."

"Jessie and Jack it shall be, then. Now, what sort of supper appeals to you at this hour of the evening? Washington isn't especially noted for its cafes, but if you've been eating in hotels, I'm sure you'll enjoy a change."

"I think I'd like something that's both light and filling," Jessie replied. "An omelet with a good sauce, perhaps?"

"Of course," Carruthers agreed. "And a bottle of champagne." He took Jessie's arm and they moved toward the door. "There's always a hack or two at the corner of the square, and Harvey's Restaurant is just a short distance away, on Eighteenth Street."

Studying her escort while they ate and sipped the sparkling wine in the big, red-draped dining room, Jessie had made her decision final with very little difficulty. Behind his careful courtesy she sensed the attraction that had drawn Carruthers to her, and as she studied his bronzed face with its rugged features, she felt a familiar stirring that told her both the man and the occasion were right.

Because of the unorthodox education Alex Starbuck had provided for her, Jessie had been prepared to live a completely full life since she'd reached a precocious maturity. The wise old geisha to whom Alex had entrusted her training had given her an attitude toward life that was far in advance of the period, and once she'd reached a decision about a man, Jessie seldom found it necessary to revise it or retreat from it.

At the same time, she'd waited for him to make the first move. The major had not disappointed her. They'd chatted about the reception while they ate the Omelettes Parisienne that the maître d'hotel had recommended, and were sipping the last of their second bottle of champagne when he switched the conversation to a more personal plane.

"Don't you find it strange, Jessie, being the only woman

14

among a number of men in such a lonely place as your ranch seems to be?" he'd asked.

"Not at all. I think the men soon stop looking on me as a woman, and just think of me as their boss."

"And they never give you any trouble?"

"Occasionally, of course. Now and then one of them will slack off in his work, and I'll have to tell my foreman to fire him. But men who are attracted to ranch life are usually a pretty good sort."

"I wasn't referring to work, Jessie," Carruthers said. "I meant personal problems."

"Making advances, things of that sort?" she asked.

"Yes. That kind of trouble."

"No. They keep their distance, I keep mine."

"And you've never been attracted to any of your workers?"

"If I have been, I've never shown it. I have my own personal life away from the ranch."

"When you're traveling, I suppose?"

"Yes."

Carruthers raised his eyebrows and locked her eyes with his as he asked, "Times like the present, I hope? When you meet somebody who's greatly attracted to you? I have been, you know, from the minute the President introduced us."

Jessie smiled. "I was wondering when you'd ask that. Yes, Jack. Times like the present."

For a moment the young officer sat silently staring at Jessie, then he said, "Now?"

"Of course."

"My flat's quite a distance away, in Georgetown. Would it embarrass you to go to a hotel with me? Willard's is just a short cab ride from here, and they're very discreet."

"Willard's happens to be where I'm staying, Jack. And it won't embarrass me a bit to invite you to my room. As

15

you say, the staff there is very discreet indeed."

In the cab on the way to Willard's, Carruthers took Jessie in his arms. She turned her face up to accept his kiss, and when his questing tongue touched her lips, she joined him in a deep, probing kiss that lasted until the carriage completed the short trip to the hotel. Hiding their eagerness, they crossed the deserted lobby and stood sedately apart in the elevator while the operator took them to the top floor, where Jessie's suite was located.

She led the way down the hall, and Carruthers followed her through the sitting room to her bedroom, on the opposite side of the suite from Ki's. A lamp on the dresser had been lighted and turned low, and it bathed the room in a dim light. Locking the door, Jessie turned to Carruthers and let her wrap slip to the floor as she opened her arms to him.

This time Carruthers did not stop his kisses at her lips. The evening gown that Jessie wore was cut low in front, and his tongue traced its way over the bulges of her breasts and into the warm hollow between them. Jessie reached over her shoulder and quickly released the top buttons, letting the gown slip down to her waist.

She threw her head back as the young officer paid tribute to her proud, upstanding breasts by taking their outthrust tips into his mouth and caressing them with his lips and tongue. By now Jessie was tingling with anticipation. She slid her hand to his crotch and began stroking the firm bulge that her fingers found there.

Looking up at her, Carruthers said, "Don't make me wait any longer, Jessie! I've been thinking all evening of being alone with you, and there's too little of the night left for us to waste time."

"You're right, Jack," she agreed. "Especially when the bed's there waiting for us."

As always, Jessie scorned fashion in her clothing. She

wore no corset, nothing except a thin silken shift and pantalettes under her dress. She let the dress and shift slide to the floor when Carruthers released her, kicked off her low-cut pumps, and then pushed down her pantalettes and hose in one deft move. She looked at Carruthers as she straightened up, naked. He'd just finished unbuttoning the long row of brass buttons of his dress uniform coat and was sitting in a chair beside the bed, his torso bare, levering off his glossy dress boots.

Smiling inwardly, but impatient nevertheless, Jessie stepped to the bed. She asked, "Would you like me to help you?"

"Damned boots do slow a man down," he told her.

"Then let's wait a few minutes to get them off," she said.

Carruthers was sitting at an angle in the chair, stretching his legs forward to rid himself of the boots. Leaning over him, Jessie quickly unbuttoned his trousers. His erection pushed up through the flap of his fly. Wordlessly, Jessie straddled him and slowly lowered herself on the rigid cylinder of firm, throbbing flesh.

"Oh Jessie, darling Jessie!" Carruthers sighed.

Bending forward to kiss him, in the moment before their lips met, Jessie said, "We can be more conventional later. Right now I'm aching to have you inside me."

"But I wanted to—"

"Hush," she whispered. "I know. There'll be time later for what you want. Right now I don't want to wait."

Their lips met, tongues intertwined, and Jessie began to rotate her hips in the motion taught her by the old geisha and refined in later years by her own experience. She moved deliberately, her inner muscles grasping her lover's rigid shaft. For a moment Carruthers tried to thrust upward, but his outstretched legs could find no leverage, and he was unable to move. After a few unsuccessful efforts he stopped trying, and let Jessie do as she wished.

Jessie did not hurry. Many weeks had passed since she'd felt drawn to a man, and the sensation that she enjoyed so fully had been amplified by her long abstinence. She moved her hips gently for several minutes before lifting herself until only the tip of Carruthers's shaft connected them, then dropped heavily to his hips. She closed her eyes, savoring the thrust that had brought a gentle shudder to her body, before repeating the lift and falling on him again.

This time she did not wait to repeat the motion, but began raising and lowering her hips faster and faster until she suddenly realized that she was bringing Carruthers to a climax. She stopped in time to delay him, and held herself pressed firmly against his crotch for several minutes, her moist warmth still engulfing him, while he tried vainly to thrust upward against her weight. Then she stood up and, before the young officer could get to his feet, grasped the toe and heel of each boot in turn and yanked them from his feet.

His eyes fixed on Jessie's nude, glowing body, Carruthers wasted no time in stepping out of his trousers and underwear. He took Jessie's hand and they moved to the bed. Jessie's preliminary lovemaking had brought him to a fever pitch of lust. He drove into the soft readiness of her body with a single lunge, and began a triphammer thrusting that started Jessie panting in rhythm with his recurring gasps, and stimulated her to respond with quick upward thrusts that matched his fierce lunges.

In spite of her ready response, Jessie held herself under control until she sensed that Carruthers had almost reached the point where he could no longer hold back. Then she let her control go, and enjoyed the mounting sensation that shook her as he carried her with him to a climax that set them both shuddering ecstatically while they exchanged soft, lingering kisses before their quivering muscles relaxed and they lay quiet.

To Jessie's pleased surprise, Carruthers turned to her again much sooner than she'd expected him to. He roused her once more with soft kisses, his lips roaming from hers to explore her breasts and lips and the even more sensitive areas of her alabaster neck and on to the most intimate areas of her body. She responded at once, matching his moves with hers, until he thrust into her once more and stroked gently for a long while before the strokes became deep, fierce lunges that went on and on until they joined in another quaking, shuddering climax.

This time the major did not leave her, but stayed until they were rested again, and then began once more to bring her to a third ecstatic peak. Dawn was showing at the edges of the drawn windowshades by now. Jessie was completely relaxed and totally satisfied as she lay beside her lover, when Carruthers stirred and propped himself up on an elbow, looking down at her.

"You're a marvelous woman, Jessie," he said in a half-whisper, stroking her soft breasts with his fingertips, his touch as gentle as the brushing of a feather. "From the little bit that the President's told me about you, I'm sure you're not like so many women, who come to Washington looking for a husband. I know you have a big ranch in Texas, and I'm sure a lot more money than I have, but I'm not exactly a pauper, and if you—"

"I'm afraid I'll have to disappoint you, Jack," Jessie replied. "Marriage isn't included in my plans."

"There's no chance your plans will change, I suppose?"

"I'm afraid not."

"Washington's an exciting place to live, you know."

Jessie smiled inwardly as she replied, "I don't think it could be home to me the way the Circle Star is. And I keep busy looking after the businesses my father built up. No, Jack, you're a wonderful lover, but marriage isn't for me."

"Will I see you again before you go?" he asked.

"I'm afraid not. My train leaves at noon, and I still have a few things to do before I leave."

"Then I suppose we'll both have to settle for what we've got now," Carruthers said. "Once again, Jessie, for memory's sake."

He turned on his side and his lips sought Jessie's. She parted her lips as the tip of his tongue touched them, and her hands became as busy caressing him as his were in stroking her warm body. They passed from first arousal through the stages of passion to another final ecstasy. Jessie lay quietly, feigning sleep, as Carruthers rose silently from the bed and dressed. She did not open her eyes when he pressed his lips gently to hers, or when she heard the click of the door as it closed behind him, but she sighed gently before falling asleep in the growing dawn.

Curled up in the big leather chair in her favorite room at the Circle Star, Jessie smiled rather than sighing as she recalled that final night in Washington. She carried memories of many men she'd encountered in her travels, and had forgotten many more, but she knew that Major Jack Carruthers would remain as one of her more pleasant reminiscences. Then the thought of her job pushed memory aside. Standing up resolutely, Jessie moved to the rolltop desk and looked at the tray on its top, overflowing with mail that had accumulated while she was in the East.

Gathering up the letters that had spilled to the desktop, Jessie replaced them on the tray and carried it to the table that stood near the leather easy chair. She began to sort the envelopes methodically, placing them in neat piles on the table. The sorting completed, Jessie looked at the dozen or more stacks of envelopes that waited to be opened. She sighed and sat down to begin.

Much of the mail she recognized as routine, fat envelopes that contained the monthly reports of operations of the varied businesses that made up the Starbuck financial-empire. These she pushed to one side; they could wait until later. Any important news from the Starbuck companies would be in separate letters, thinner than those dealing with routine matters.

There were still more than two dozen thin envelopes when she'd finished weeding out the routine items. Since she'd just returned from the East, Jessie decided that she'd already be familiar with their contents. She picked up the envelopes with Western postmarks and sat down, but had just opened the first of the letters when the latch of the study door clicked and she looked around. Ki stood in the doorway.

"Ki!" she exclaimed. "You startled me. I thought you were going to bed. What's the matter? Can't you sleep?"

"Things may not be as peaceful as we thought."

"What do you mean?"

"Someone must have been waiting for us to get back to the ranch, Jessie," he said quietly. "A noise woke me up a few minutes ago. I thought at first that it was you closing your bedroom door, then I heard it again and looked out the window. There's somebody prowling around the house."

"Oh no, Ki! Not again!"

"I'm afraid so, Jessie. I watched long enough to make sure it wasn't one of our own hands. I can recognize them in the dark, even when I can't see their faces, by the way they walk and hold their bodies."

"I should've heard hoofbeats, on a night as quiet as this," Jessie said, frowning. "There hasn't been a sound, though."

21

"If I was sneaking up on someone, I'd leave my horse a long way from where I expected to find my quarry," Ki pointed out.

"Are you sure there's only one man?"

"One man is here now. That doesn't mean there aren't others waiting for him to call them up to the house."

"True." Jessie nodded. "Alex always warned me that the cartel never sleeps and never gives up. He was right about that, just as he was about so many other things."

"It's a little bit early for the cartel to move against us for stopping their latest attack on your banks, Jessie," Ki said thoughtfully.

"Not necessarily. Remember, we stayed in Washington for two days after we left New York. And the East Coast isn't any farther away for them than it is for us."

"Perhaps we'd better not jump to conclusions. It might be someone who wandered off the trail in the dark, and wound up here by mistake."

Jessie shook her head. "Not likely. But before we do anything, let's get our rifles out of the gun rack and go upstairs where we can get a better view. We'll know soon enough whether the prowler is a friend or an enemy."

Chapter 3

There were windows at each end of the hallway that divided the second floor of the Circle Star's main house into approximately equal halves, as well as windows in the bedrooms on either side of the hall. Carrying the rifles they'd taken from the gun rack beside the front door, Jessie and Ki hurried up the stairs. Jessie pointed to the doors of the corner bedrooms. These rooms had windows that would give them views of both the ends and the sides of the rambling ranch house.

Jessie signaled to Ki to take his room at the far end of the hall, and pointed to the room at the opposite end, then to herself. Having shared the dangers of so many brushes with the cartel's gunmen, they needed no other signals. Ki moved down the hall in one direction, Jessie in the other.

For a moment after she peered from the almost pitch blackness of the room into the lesser blackness outside, Jessie could see nothing. Then her eyes adjusted to the changed light, and the familiar shapes of the Circle Star's bunkhouse and kitchen became visible, while beyond it she could make out a corner of the horse corral.

At first she could see no movement, and was getting ready to turn away from the window and join Ki when a flicker of motion in the area between the dark bunkhouse and the corral caught her eyes. As she concentrated on the spot, the dark figure of a moving man came into focus in the bare space. Jessie started to raise her rifle, but thought better of the idea before she'd shouldered the weapon. In the darkness and the distance, the moving form might well be one of the hands, for at that distance all moving shadows tended to look alike.

She heard Ki's footsteps, his rope-soled sandals moving almost inaudibly on the hall floor, and turned as he came into the room.

"I didn't see the prowler this time," Ki said. "But that doesn't mean he's gone."

"He's not," Jessie replied. "I can see him from this window now. He's standing between the bunkhouse and corral, but I can't decide what he's planning to do."

"He might be trying to steal a horse from the corral," Ki suggested.

"That's possible. But he's had plenty of time to take a horse and be on his way since you first saw him."

"You're sure it's not one of our men?" Ki asked. "I didn't recognize him, but it's not easy to make out details in the darkness."

"Quite sure. He's a big man, about the size of Ed Wright, but we know Ed's with the market herd. Let's go downstairs and find out. We'll have the advantage of surprise if we plan our moves carefully."

"Suppose you stay here and keep an eye on him," Ki suggested. "I'll slip out the back door and circle around behind the bunkhouse. When I'm in place, you go out the front door and come up on the opposite side. I'll wait until you're in place, then we'll have him between us."

"Go ahead," Jessie said. "I'll start as soon as I see you go behind the corner of the bunkhouse."

She turned back to the window. The intruder had not

moved; he was still standing between the bunkhouse and corral. Ki came into sight, angling toward the corner of the bunkhouse, keeping the building's bulk between himself and the prowler. He moved with the silence he'd learned during his samurai training, his soft shoes making no sound as he advanced carefully over the baked earth.

When Ki reached the bunkhouse, Jessie left her observation post and hurried down the stairs. She circled the main house and stopped at its back corner. The man was still standing where he'd been the last time she looked out the window. Bringing her rifle up to where she could choose between snapshooting from her hip or shouldering the gun for an aimed shot, Jessie stepped from the shielding corner of the house and started toward the intruder.

She'd covered about half the distance when she saw Ki break cover and emerge from behind the bunkhouse. He was within a dozen paces of the prowler, and Jessie judged that the time had come for a showdown. Making no effort to move silently, she stepped from her cover with her rifle at her hip, leveled at the intruder.

"Don't move!" she called quickly. "Keep your hands still and stand quietly!"

To her surprise, the man obeyed. A shadowy figure in the moonless night, he did not turn his head or move his hands, and made no effort to run. Ki stopped a bit more than arm's length from him, and Jessie quickly closed the distance to take a similar position. She could still see very little detail. The stranger's face was cast into a dark shadow by the wide brim of his hat. It was not the type of hat worn by cowhands, Jessie noted in the few seconds of observation she allowed herself.

"Suppose you tell us who you are," Jessie went on. "And what you're doing prowling around here in the middle of the night."

Instead of answering her directly, the stranger replied with a question. "Are you Miss Jessie Starbuck?"

Jessie did not lower the rifle muzzle as she answered, "Yes. You must know that, though, or you wouldn't be here."

"You have nothing to fear from me, Miss Starbuck," the man said. "I'm sorry I have caused you worry. It was my plan to get her in daylight, but in this strange land of great distances I misjudged the distance and the time it would take me to reach your ranch."

"You still haven't answered my question," Jessie told him sternly. "I want to know your name and where you're from before I lower this rifle. And I want some proof that you're telling me the truth when you do answer."

"My name in your language is Standing Bear," the stranger replied. "In my own tongue it is Hitaze Noka."

Ki asked, "You are an Indian, then?"

"Truly so, brother. And you? *Waenaesh k'dodaem?*"

Ki's frown was visible to Jessie even in the darkness. They were both familiar with the cadence and intonation of the Cheyenne and Pueblo and Apache languages, but the words the stranger spoke were not rooted in any of those.

Ki told the man, "I don't understand your language."

"But you look like one of us," Standing Bear said. "What is your totem, then?"

"My name is Ki, but I'm not Indian," Ki replied. "My native home is not this country, but one far across the ocean."

Jessie broke in a bit impatiently to say, "You're still not answering my questions, Standing Bear. Where did you come from, and why are you here looking for me? Obviously you know where you are, and I can understand how you could have misjudged your distance in planning the time you'd get here, and how you might be familiar with my

26

name. But I want to know a lot more before I let this rifle down."

"Please trust me, Miss Starbuck," Standing Bear said. "I am truly sorry I have disturbed your rest. It was because I did not want to do this thing that I have caused you trouble. I was looking for a place where I could sleep until morning, and greet you in the daylight. It is a bad thing that you saw me and mistook my intentions."

"How can I be sure you're telling the truth?" Jessie asked.

"I will show you proof, when there is light enough."

Ki broke in to ask, "What's your tribe, Standing Bear? It can't be one of the Western tribes, or you'd know how to judge travel distances better."

"I am of the Zaugee. We are the people of the river mouths far to the east of here, where the Great Mother River begins. Our lands are around the Great Shining Waters. The whites call us Ojibway, which is our true name, though sometimes now they say we are Chippewa."

There was a ring of truth about Standing Bear's words, which convinced Jessie that he was not lying. She asked him, "And you've come all this way to find me?"

"Yes, Miss Starbuck. It's a great distance, much farther than I or my chiefs understood. We knew the land was big, but we did not know how big."

"We'd better go inside," Jessie said decisively. "If we stand here talking much longer, we're going to wake up the hands in the bunkhouse. Come on, Standing Bear. I'm curious to find out what brought you here."

Jessie led the way toward the main house, and Ki walked beside Standing Bear a few paces behind her. Jessie glanced over her shoulder at the pair, and for the first time realized how tall and broad the Ojibway man really was. He towered above Ki, and was twice as broad. Ki noticed the other man's halting gait.

27

"How did you get to the Circle Star?" he asked the Indian. "I didn't hear a horse. Did you walk all the way from the railroad?"

"From the railroad and along it, yes."

"Across the desert, on foot?"

"Of course." Standing Bear's voice showed no surprise. He added, "I am not a stranger to badlands, Ki. There are places as bad as those I crossed in the land of the Dakotas, which is near the place I live."

"But why didn't you come all the way on the train?"

"My ticket brought me only to the last big town, so I followed the rails on foot for many miles."

"Something close to fifty miles, if you walked from the last good-sized town. Didn't you know there was a whistle stop at the spur that we ship Circle Star cattle from?"

"A long distance separates this place from my home, Ki. The elders and I did not understand how far I would have to travel. They gave me what we thought was a great deal of money, but I have already used all I had."

"When did you eat last?"

"Yesterday morning," Standing Bear replied, his voice quite casual.

"Jessie," Ki said as they reached the house, "you go on into the study with Standing Bear. I'm going to fix something for him to eat. He's been walking for two whole days."

"Without food and water?" Jessie asked.

"Oh, I had water," Standing Bear said. "There were the big tanks for the trains along the way."

"You're lucky it's not midsummer," Jessie told the Ojibway. "You'd be dead if you'd tried to walk like that a month or two from now."

"It was not pleasant," Standing Bear said thoughtfully. "But it was not all bad. I have seen things that I might not have noticed if I had been traveling fast. In the place where

28

I live, there are not such things as I have looked at here. I have many questions that I must ask someone. Perhaps you, Jessie Starbuck."

"We'll talk about the land later," Jessie said firmly. "I want to know first why you came here."

"To tell you and to explain everything will take time. Will you let me eat first, please? Suddenly I am very hungry."

Jessie needed no proof that the Ojibway had suffered from his desert trip on foot, in spite of the casual way in which he spoke of it. In the light of the coal-oil lamp that burned in the study, she could see now that his face was seamed with fine wrinkles that sagged into deep lines because of his hunger and dehydration.

Chiding herself mentally for her failure to realize his condition, she motioned Standing Bear to sit down. He lowered himself into the sofa, and as though the thought of resting had relaxed the tension he'd been under for so many days, he seemed to grow smaller as he fell back against the supporting cushions.

"I'm sorry," she said. "I didn't realize what bad shape you were in. Rest, by all means. Ki will be here soon with some food and coffee."

Going to her own favorite chair, Jessie sat down and looked at the weary man. She found it impossible to estimate his age. If the seams that showed on his bronzed face were the result of dehydration, he could be in his early or middle forties, but if the lines denoted age, he might well be sixty, she decided.

Standing Bear's nose was thin and aquiline, and jutted from his brows like the beak of a predatory bird, an eagle or a hawk, not wide and flat like the noses of the Western tribesmen with whom Jessie was most familiar. His cheeks were sunken now, hollows between high cheekbones and a broad jawline. His lips were thin, his chin square. His eyes,

29

like the eyes of most of the Indians Jessie knew, were deep black under thin brows, and almost opaque.

Jessie was so absorbed in her study of Standing Bear's face that she did not realize he was scrutinizing her as closely as she was studying him. The Ojibway spoke suddenly.

"Yes," he said decisively. "You are the daughter of Alex Starbuck. Though I was only a young man when he stayed among my people, I remember him well. I think I might have known you if we had met anywhere."

Jessie frowned. "I didn't know my father had spent any time in your part of the country."

"There are many things that parents do not tell children," Standing Bear reminded her. "Perhaps your father forgot, or did not see the need to tell you of his visit with my people."

"Alex wouldn't forget, Standing Bear," Jessie said positively. "But as you said, he may have had some reason for not mentioning it to me."

"It was in a time long past," the Indian said. "Few of our people still live who were alive when the trouble came upon us, but all of us know from our elders that the sky was black with evil for many years."

"What was Alex doing when he visited you?" Jessie asked.

"He was making boards from trees. There was a sawmill near our villages, and he had bought it. He needed more trees, and we welcomed his need. We were not makers of boards or weapons. We were hunters and fishermen, we traded meat and fish and hides with the Hurons and other tribes for grain."

"And do you still trade with them?"

Standing Bear shook his head. "In the Land of Shining Water we are no longer hunters and fishermen and traders. Now we are farmers. We sell our grain to the buyers of

30

wheat and corn who come from the East."

Ki came in from the kitchen, carrying a platter on which was piled a steaming heap of rice mixed with vegetables and shreds of ham. He gave the platter and a fork to Standing Bear, saying, "This is the quickest meal I could think of. But it'll stop your hunger until breakfast tomorrow."

"Thank you, Ki," the Ojibway said. "It is much like a dish our tribe knows. We are rice-gatherers, too, you know."

"No, I didn't know," Ki replied. "In fact, I don't know a great deal about the Indian people east of the Mississippi."

Standing Bear's mouth was full, and he could only nod in agreement. After he'd finished chewing and swallowing, he said, "Our brothers here in the West were left to themselves by the white man until just a short time ago. We of the Eastern tribes have dealt with them for four hundred years. But I have heard that now their way of life is changing, just as ours began to change those many years ago."

"All the Eastern tribes are at peace with one another now, aren't they?" Jessie asked.

Again Standing Bear's reply was delayed, then he said, "We are at peace, but old memories die hard. My people have not yet forgotten or forgiven the time when the Mohawk and Onondaga and Seneca drove us west from our tribal lands."

"Then you haven't always lived around the Great Lakes?" Jessie asked.

Standing Bear shook his head. "No. We were attacked by the tribes who had been our brothers, because their lands were being taken from them by the white men. Now we live in peace with them again, but we do not forget or forgive."

"How long ago was that, Standing Bear?" Ki asked.

"More years than a man can remember," the Ojibway answered. "It was when the Eastern tribes divided between

31

your leader in Washington and the British king over the ocean."

"More than a hundred years ago?" Jessie frowned. "And you still aren't really friends again?"

"And will never be," the Ojibway said firmly. He fell silent until he'd cleaned the last bits of food off his platter, then went on, "But I did not come here to talk of our past troubles, Jessie Starbuck."

"Why did you come?" Jessie asked.

"Because of the troubles we are having now."

"And why? Because my father told you he'd help you if you ever needed him?"

Standing Bear's eyes opened wide in surprise, then a frown grew on his wrinkled face. He asked Jessie, "How do you know this, if you did not know your father had stayed with us?"

"Because it's the sort of thing Alex would have done. My father was an honest and generous man."

"Yes," the Indian broke in. "Of this I have been told by the old men of our people, those who knew him."

"Whenever someone helped Alex, he considered it a debt to be repaid," Jessie went on. "And I've always tried to make good on his promises, just as he'd have done if he was still alive."

"Then you will keep your father's word?" Standing Bear's frown cleared like magic and he added, "It is a good thing of which you tell me, Jessie Starbuck. You are worthy of your father's name."

"Don't assume too much, Standing Bear," Jessie cautioned. "I'll want to hear what your trouble is, and why it's so big that you feel you had to come here looking for help."

"It will be easier to tell you why than to explain our trouble," Standing Bear said. "We came because we know that we can trust one who carries the Starbuck name. What

32

I must tell you is much more than what you think, Jessie Starbuck. You must hear all of it to understand, and now that my belly is full, I am very tired."

"And you'd like to wait until tomorrow to tell me the whole story?" she asked. When the Ojibway nodded, Jessie went on, "I don't mind waiting. Ki and I have had a long day too."

"I'll fix one of the spare bedrooms for him, Jessie," Ki volunteered. "All three of us need sleep right now."

Standing Bear said quickly, "Before you sleep, Jessie Starbuck, I must show you the proof you need that your father did indeed live among our people. You will sleep better if you know I tell you no lies."

"All right." Jessie nodded. "Whatever papers you have, I'll look at them now, and if you'll trust me with them, I'll study them carefully before we talk tomorrow."

"Oh, I have no papers. Few of us could read and write well when your father was among us," Standing Bear told her. "But I have a token that endures better than paper."

Fumbling at his throat, the Ojibway pulled at a thong and produced a small bucksin bag from beneath his shirt. He opened the bag and shook it over his upturned palm. A gold signet ring fell out. Silently, Standing Bear handed the ring to Jessie.

Jessie looked at the heavy golden circlet. On its wide back the initials *A.S.* had been engraved in antiquated script. She stepped closer to the lamp and looked at the inner surface of the band.

There, in tiny letters, she saw a facsimile of her father's signature: *Alex Starbuck*.

★

Chapter 4

"My father gave this ring to you?" she asked Standing Bear.

Shaking his head, the Ojibway replied, "Not to me, but to my people. It has been in the keeping of our medicine chief. I was too young to be a member of our tribe's council when Alex Starbuck left the ring as a pledge to return if we should need his help again."

"How long ago was that, Standing Bear?" Ki asked. "I was with Alex for many years, and this is the first time I've heard about the ring."

"I do not know the answer to your question, Ki," Standing Bear replied soberly. "I was told there was a token, but until I was chosen to bring you the message from my people, I did not know the token was a ring. I saw it for the first time when our medicine chief gave it to me before I left to come here."

"Alex must have been very young when he was with your tribe, then," Jessie frowned.

"Our medicine chief told me that he himself was little more than a boy. Always our people have thought that wisdom comes only with age, but Alex Starbuck convinced them of his wisdom even when he was very young. But the elders of our tribe asked him if he would promise them on his totem to return, and it was then that he left the ring as his pledge."

"Pledge?" Jessie asked. "What did he pledge?"

"That is what I have come to tell you of, Jessie Starbuck," Standing Bear said. "But we have agreed, you and I, that we will wait until tomorrow to talk of these things."

"Of course," Jessie said. "We're both tired, and I'm getting sleepier by the minute. We'll have our talk tomorrow, when our heads are clear."

"That is my wish too," Standing Bear replied. "In my youth, I could make a walk such as I just finished, and play games with my friends at its end. But that was years ago. Now I think only of bed and sleep."

On a sudden impulse, Jessie asked, "Will you let me keep the ring overnight? I'll give it back to you tomorrow."

The Ojibway nodded. "Of course. The ring is a message as well as a totem. Perhaps while you sleep it will give you the message Alex Starbuck wanted it to carry."

Ki broke in. "Come along, Standing Bear. I'll show you where your room is." Then he asked, "Jessie, are you coming to bed now?"

"Yes, of course. Go ahead, Ki. I'll blow out the light as soon as you and Standing Bear are upstairs."

When she heard the faint sound of doors closing on the upper floor, Jessie blew out the lamp and went upstairs in the darkness. She did not light the lamp in her bedroom, but let her clothes fall to the floor and went to bed at once. She fell asleep immediately, still clutching the ring in her hand.

Jessie woke with a start in the darkness, aware of a pain on one side of her face. She brushed her hand between her head and the pillow and discovered that the cause of the

35

discomfort was Alex's ring, which had slipped from her hand and lodged beneath her cheek. She pulled the ring away and placed it on her bedside table, then closed her eyes, expecting to go back to sleep at once. Now that she'd been awakened, though, sleep would not return. Thoughts of the night filled her mind, the arrival of Standing Bear, his untold story, the ring that had belonged to Alex.

For what seemed a long time, Jessie lay motionless, staring at the starlit night, which turned the windows of her room into pale rectangles against the inner darkness. When sleep continued to elude her, Jessie sighed and got out of bed. Her nude body a white shadow in the dark room, she stepped to her wardrobe chest and felt along the hangers until she found her silk lounging robe. Slipping her arms into it, she tied the sash and ran her hand over the top of the bedside table until she found the ring. Then she went downstairs into the study.

Still holding the ring in one hand, Jessie's first move after lighting the lamp was to the safe that stood in a corner of the room. She dialed the combination and swung open the heavy door. Reaching for the knob of one of the small compartments that filled the upper third of the interior, she opened it and took out a velvet jeweler's box.

Carrying the box to the table where the lamp stood, Jessie put the ring brought by Standing Bear on the table and opened the jeweler's box. Setting her jaw and blanking unhappy memories from her mind, she took out the signet ring Alex had been wearing at the time of his murder by the cartel's hired gunmen. Then she picked up the ring that Standing Bear had given her and put it beside the one she was already holding.

Moving her hand with the two rings under the lampshade where the light was brightest, she examined them closely. Except for individual scratches and signs of wear, the rings

36

were identical. Each bore the deeply incised letters *A.S.* on the flat surface, and each had *Alex Starbuck* engraved in script on the inside of the band.

Jessie's curiosity was still unsatisfied. She laid the rings on the table and returned to the safe, where she took the earliest volumes of her father's diaries from the compartment where she kept them, and carried them to her favorite chair. Settling back against the smooth leather, cool now in the night, she began thumbing through the small, dog-eared books in which Alex had kept a running account of his days.

In the first few pages of the second book, Jessie found the entry she was seeking: *From Chicago to Winnipeg fol' wg rumor large timber tract on market. Discovered timberland owned by Ojibway Indians. Distrustul of whites. Buying may not be easy.* There were three pages missing from the book following the brief memorandum, then, on an otherwise blank page, she read the cryptic notation *Treasure River.*

Jessie turned the page quickly, confident that she would find further details, but there was no further reference to a river or to timberland, or to the Ojibways. She skimmed through the remainder of the diary, but found nothing more than the routine notes of Alex's return to San Francisco.

Remembering that in his earliest diaries Alex often made only sketchy notes of his activities, rather than including small details such as he'd done in later years after his business interests became more complex, Jessie went back to the safe and took out the ledger that covered the period of the diary. She went through the ledger line by line until she found the entry she'd been looking for: *To Kayaushk, on behalf Ojibway tribe, $11,000 gld.*

Though she went through the ledger to the final page, there was no record of a withdrawal of the sum paid to the

37

Ojibways, no credit against receipts from the sale of timber, no debit that accounted for the $11,000 paid out.

Bewildered and frustrated, Jessie returned the diary and ledger to the safe. She picked up the rings. Only her memory could tell her the differences between them. She returned the second ring to its box and replaced it in the safe. She left the ring brought by Standing Bear on the table.

Still trying to fathom the mysteries of the missing ledger entries and the pages torn from the diary, Jessie blew out the lamp and returned to her room. In bed again, she went to sleep at once and did not awaken until she heard Ki going down the stairway shortly after sunup. She lay quietly for a few minutes, then rose and took from the wardrobe the clothes she always wore at the Circle Star, dressed quickly, and went downstairs.

"We're getting a late start this morning," Ki greeted her as she entered the kitchen. A covered cast-iron skillet was on the kitchen range, and Ki was standing at the chopping block, cutting slices from a ham.

"I suppose I needed the extra sleep, Ki. I didn't even heary Gimpy call the hands to breakfast."

"That's what roused me. I decided I might as well cook breakfast, as long as I was awake. All I could find was ham and potatoes. I hope that suits you."

"Since you're cooking, I won't find fault with the menu. But why didn't you call Standing Bear and me? We could have had breakfast with the hands."

"I don't think we'd have had much chance to eat, Jessie. When I talked to the men yesterday, they kept me busy answering questions about what we'd seen and done while we were in the East. What really caught their fancy was your dinner at the White House with President Hayes and his wife."

"That was the dinner you excused yourself from attend-

38

ing." Jessie smiled and asked, "How did you fill in the gaps?"

"Oh, you'd told me enough about it so that I had all the details I needed to satisfy them. But I think if you get another invitation, I'll change my mind about going with you."

"You'd have been welcome to go too, you know."

"Yes," Ki said. "But it didn't seem such a good idea at the time. If you remember, I went with you to one of Mr. Hayes's dinners once, and really didn't enjoy it too much."

Jessie said thoughtfully, "To tell you the truth, Ki, I didn't enjoy it so much myself. Mr. Hayes doesn't do a great deal of talking, and Mrs. Hayes is so interested in telling everyone about the evils of liquor that I found it a little boring myself. If Major Carruthers hadn't been there, I think I might have dozed off."

"Those friends of Alex's we talked to in New York were a lot more interesting. John D. Rockefeller and Andrew Carnegie and Jay Gould."

"But you'd met them before, too."

"Not all of them. Carnegie was the only one I'd met when Alex was alive. But the way his ideas have changed since I met him with Alex interested me. And bothered me a little, too."

"Bothered you? How?"

"Exactly the same way that Rockefeller's and Gould's ideas did, because they're all so much alike."

"Getting bigger all the time, no matter what it costs or how much harm it does to others?" Jessie asked. When Ki nodded soberly, she went on, "I noticed that too. So did Alex, the first time he took me with him on his Eastern trips."

"Alex changed, though, after he found out about the cartel and its plans. He realized that enough money was enough, and began spending his profits, fighting the cartel to keep it from taking over the country," Ki said.

"Maybe the others will change too," Jessie suggested. "He kept hoping some of his friends would, but he didn't tell them about the cartel because he felt there was a danger they might join it."

"I suppose we can always hope," Ki said. He took the skillet off the stove and emptied the ham slices onto the platter. "If you'll set the table, I'll go wake Standing Bear. After what he went through getting here, I'm sure he'll be glad to eat again."

"What did you make of his story, Ki?"

"It sounded true enough to me. And he had Alex's ring to back it up."

"Oh, I wasn't talking about that," Jessie said quickly. "Though I did look at the ring Alex was wearing when— when he was killed. It's almost identical to the one Standing Bear has."

"Yes. I could tell that last night."

"And making the kind of promise Standing Bear mentioned is exactly the sort of thing Alex would have done," Jessie went on thoughtfully.

"Alex would never make a promise he wasn't positive he could keep," Ki said thoughtfully. "But there's something missing from Standing Bear's story, Jessie."

Unexpectedly, Standing Bear himself spoke from the doorway. "Of course there is, Ki. I have not finished telling you the whole story, but even when I do, there will still be something missing. This is a thing I do not know myself, but Migizi has promised that he will tell you when the time is right."

"Whatever it is that's missing must be very important," Jessie said. "But let's eat breakfast before we start talking about what you've come here for."

"Good. I will talk better when my stomach is full again,"

the Ojibway replied. "Even after all I ate last night, I am hungry again this morning."

They sat down to breakfast in the dining room, and during the meal they talked of other things than Standing Bear's mission. Both Jessie and Ki were curious about Ojibway tribal history, and about the country that the tribe called its homeland. All of them carefully avoided talking of the purpose of his visit until the big platter was empty and they'd each had a final cup of coffee.

"Shall we talk now, Jessie Starbuck?" Standing Bear asked.

"Yes. Ki will be with us, unless you want me to be the only one to know why you're here," she said.

"You would tell him what we talked about if he did not hear it himself, would you not?" the Ojibway asked.

"Of course, if you didn't ask me not to."

"Then let him hear my words as I speak them to you. It will be better that way."

They moved into the study and sat for a moment in a formal and slightly awkward silence until Standing Bear began.

"First I must ask you this thing, Jessie Starbuck. Do you believe what I told you last night, of the promise your father made our people? The promise he left his gold ring to pledge?"

"Of course I do, Standing Bear. But I'd like to know why Alex made such a promise, and why you've come here to ask me to honor his pledge."

"Let me tell you what happened before Alex Starbuck came to our people," Standing Bear said. "This was long ago, you understand. We Ojibway first had our lands north of the five big, shining waters which you call the Great Lakes. Then the Iroquois tribes were pushed west by the white men from across the ocean, and they were stronger

41

than the Algonkin, and the Algonkin were stronger than the Ojibway. So the Algonkin took the Ojibway lands and drove us south. And there between the big waters we lived many years. But still the whites pushed from the East, and the Algonkin made war on our people. And they were the stronger fighters, and pushed us ahead of them. So, when my great-great-grandfather was a boy, our people were forced to move again."

"And this place where you settled the second time was where you were when Alex came to your tribe?" Jessie asked.

Standing Bear nodded. "Yes. It was at the south end of the lake that now is called Winnipeg. Already the Hudson's Bay men had hunted and trapped there until game was scarce. We had to learn to plant and harvest grain, and our people were no longer hunters. Even when my grandfather was a boy, we had become farmers."

"You're telling us an interesting story, but I don't see what it has to do with Alex's pledge to your tribe," Jessie said, the beginning of a frown showing on her face.

"Please be patient," the Ojibway said. "You will see now why what I have told you is necessary for you to understand everything that has followed."

Jessie nodded, and Standing Bear went on, "When my people moved for the third time, we were no longer on land won by your General Washington from the Englishmen. We did not understand then what we learned later, that in Canada land must be bought by Indians as well as whites."

"I can't understand that," Jessie broke in. "In the United States, the government always gave lands to the Indians who were forced to relocate."

"Perhaps not quite always," Standing Bear said gently. "But most of the time it did. In Canada it was not the same. We learned too late that there we were squatters."

42

"So," Ki said, "when Alex came to you and offered to buy your timberland, you found you had no land to sell him?"

"Even worse," Standing Bear said. "We Ojibway found that we did not even own the lands on which we had settled. It had much value by then, after we had spent so many years clearing it and proving it would produce good crops."

"That's where Alex helped you?" Jessie asked.

"More than we expected he would," Standing Bear replied. "You must understand that we had no money. But Alex Starbuck saw the injustice that we were suffering, even though it was our own foolishness that was at its root. He paid the Canadian government for the farmlands and timberlands we had thought were ours, then offered to return the land to us if our people cut the trees and gave them to him."

"And then you had all the land to farm." Jessie smiled and went on, "It sounds like the sort of thing Alex would have done. He hated injustice as much as he hated dishonesty. But if you own your farms now, why have you come here for help?"

"Because now there are men trying to steal from us the land that Alex Starbuck let us earn," Standing Bear replied, his voice sober.

"How can they steal land?" Jessie asked.

"It is hard to explain, for their stealing is very cleverly done. They do not do it openly, but make it look like something else."

"I'm afraid I don't understand," Jessie said.

"Let me try to explain it to you," Standing Bear replied. "In the past month, three Ojibway farmers have died in accidents that should not have happened. Then men came to the families of those who died and offered to buy their farms. Two have been sold."

43

"That doesn't sound too unusual, Standing Bear," Jessie said thoughtfully. "A family might want to sell a place that would have unhappy memories for them."

"Wait, there is more. The farms that were sold were at the headwaters of large streams. The buyers diverted the water so that the farms downstream are dry. Then men came and offered to buy the farms that lack of water had made worthless. Can you explain this, Jessie Starbuck?"

Jessie was silent for a moment, then she said, "That does sound like a pattern is forming. But suspecting is one thing, proof is another. Have you been able to find any proof that the accidents were murder? Or that the new owners of the two farms are acting together?"

Standing Bear shook his head. "No. We have gone to the mounted police, and they ask what you have just asked, 'Can you prove what you suspect?' And we cannot do this."

Ki broke in with a question. "Isn't there an agency in Canada like the Indian Bureau in this country, Standing Bear? A government bureau that protects Indian rights?"

Shaking his head, the Ojibway replied, "No, Ki. I know of the Indian Bureau in your country, but in Canada we are all alike, Indian or white. We have no guardian in the government to protect us."

"Has this—this plot you suspect been going on very long?" Jessie asked. "Or is it something new?"

"I think it has been happening for a longer time than we have realized," Standing Bear replied slowly. "The land-grabbers are very clever men. They move slowly, and for a long while we did not see the pattern of what was taking place. But there have been other accidents and other farms sold before, though not as close together as the three I just told you of."

"Why would they go to such a lot of trouble to get your farmland, though?" Jessie went on. "Surely there's enough land in Canada that's unsettled to satisfy anybody who wants to buy a farm."

"This has puzzled us too. And we have not found an answer to your question. That is why I have come to you, Jessie Starbuck."

"What do you expect me to do, Standing Bear?"

"That is something I do not know. I was chosen by my elders on the council to come here and tell you what we suspect, and ask you to honor Alex Starbuck's promise to help us."

She said slowly, "All right, Standing Bear. We'll rest another day here at the ranch. Then Ki and I will go with you and see if we can find out what's really going on."

Chapter 5

"This Red River certainly doesn't remind me of the one in Texas, Ki," Jessie said. "It's flowing in the wrong direction. I keep thinking we're going south to the Gulf of Mexico instead of north toward Canada."

"It's a big big river," Ki agreed. "The Texas Red River's just a little creek compared to this one."

"So many new towns and farms along it, too," Jessie went on. "I hadn't any idea this part of the country was being settled so fast."

"You will see the river grow much bigger before we end our journey," Standing Bear said. "But there will not be so many farms and towns. The new settlers have not come in such numbers to Canada, but they will arrive when the rails are laid farther to the north."

They'd found railroad travel to be impractical after reaching the northern tier of states. With the Northern Pacific barely out of bankruptcy, and the St. Paul & Pacific in the process of being swallowed by the ambitious Jim Hill, rail traffic for hundreds of miles along the border between the United States and Canada was at a virtual standstill. At Standing Bear's suggestion, they'd gotten off the train at Fargo and booked passage on the first northbound passenger boat on the Red River of the North.

Jessie had been surprised to see that the sidewheel riverboat was so large. The *Northern Queen* had twin smokestacks amidships, and two tiers of cabins above the main decks where the dining room and main salon were located, between the fore and aft cargo areas. She and Ki and Standing Bear had just come out of the dining room after supper and were standing on the second deck, watching dusk's swift approach.

"When do we cross the Canadian border?" Jessie asked.

"Tomorrow night," the Ojibway replied. "Then we have only one more day and night before we get to Winnipeg, and another day before our travel is finished."

While they were at dinner, lamps had been lighted in some of the cabins as well as in the dining room and the main salon. Now the tinkle of a piano and the sharper plunking of a banjo being tuned came from the salon.

"If you and Ki would like to dance, there will be music for an hour or two," Standing Bear said.

"That doesn't appeal to me tonight, Standing Bear," Jessie replied. "The thought of bed attracts me a lot more strongly."

"I think I agree with Jessie about dancing," Ki said. "But I'm not sleepy yet." He cocked his head toward the salon when the banjo player strummed a chord across his now-tuned strings, and went on, "Standing Bear, would you like to go into the salon with me and watch the dancers and listen to the music for a little while?"

"No," the Ojibway answered. "I don't understand the kind of music they play. It is not like that which I have learned."

"Then I'll go in and watch and listen for a few minutes," Ki said as the first strains of music sounded. "I think I caught up on my sleep last night."

Except for the trio of musicians—pianist, banjo player,

47

and trombonist—the salon was almost deserted. Three couples, all middle-aged, sat in the chairs along the walls; from their dress and appearance, Ki took them to be from farms on the steamer's route. A man wearing a derby and a tight, city-style suit stood at one side of the band, beating time with an extended forefinger. Another man had settled into a chair across the room, and a woman wearing a white serge coat-suit and a matching white straw hat occupied one of the chairs.

Ki chose a seat close to the door and sat down. He recognized the passengers from having seen them in the dining room, and apparently they'd noticed him as well, for aside from casual glances, those already in the salon paid no attention to him. Leaning back comfortably, Ki listened to the music while he watched the trio of players.

As the *Northern Queen*'s passengers were drawn by the music, the salon gradually grew more crowded. The musicians switched to a waltz, and a pair of dancers took the floor. Their example drew another couple, then a third and a fourth, until the trio began to play a new tune that had a faster beat and two of the dancing couples went back to their seats.

Ki watched the ebb and flow of couples on the dance floor for perhaps a half hour before deciding that he'd heard and seen enough for the evening. He went outside to the deck, deserted now in the darkness. Except for the reflection of the boat's running lights on the river's night-black surface, Ki might well have been looking into empty space. Apparently there were no towns along this section of the stream, and no farms either, for not a glimmer of light could be seen anywhere, on either side of the river's banks.

Staring at blackness held no attraction for Ki; he decided that a walk around the boat's perimeter might make him feel like sleeping. Strolling along at a slow pace, he reached the wide sliding doors of the forward cargo compartment and stopped for a few minutes to watch the crew moving boxes and bales to the deck, getting them in place at the gangplank to be unloaded swiftly at the next stop.

After a circuit of the main deck, Ki reached the stairs that led to the upper decks, and for lack of anything better to do, he mounted them to the top, where he stopped again at the wheelhouse. For a moment or so he gazed into the little cubicle's dimly lighted interior at the pilot and steersman, their eyes focused intently through the wide, glassed-in front window at the river's surface, a slick black shimmer in the moonless night.

Thinking of the complexities of piloting a steamboat the size of the *Northern Queen* up a winding river in the darkness, Ki stopped at the wheel housing and looked down at the white froth of wash created by the paddles as they churned the water.

For a moment he wondered why the foaming bubbles did not stream out in the wake of the steamboat, then realized that the vessel was moving with the current rather than against it, which reduced its wake to a thin line at the stern. His eyes moved back along the surface to the paddles, and a hint of something odd caught his keen vision. Another boat, smaller than the *Northern Queen* and propelled by oars, was approaching the steamer at an angle that would bring it to the passenger vessel's side, between the wheel and the stern.

His interest caught by the idea of the boats meeting in midstream, Ki watched the approaching craft. His sharp eyes quickly adjusted to the blackness of the night, and he began to pick out details of the smaller boat as it came closer. Then his interest changed from casual observation to concern, and as the men in the approaching boat did not hail the *Northern Queen* to call for its crew to look for a boarding line, his concern became alarm.

By now Ki could see that the smaller, unlighted vessel, which had already gotten to within a few yards of the steamboat's side, was packed with men. The bow of the approaching craft swung as its steersman began to bring it to a course that would intercept the steamboat.

Lights from the *Northern Queen* washed across the small craft as it maneuvered closer, and Ki saw the glint of steel. He narrowed his eyes to focus them better, and now he could see that the glints came from the barrels of rifles and shotguns which most of the men in the boat were holding.

Ki's swift reflexes sent him into action instantly. He ran around the side of the *Northern Queen* opposite the small boat, and burst into the pilot house. The pilot and steersman stared at him in surprise as he stopped just inside the door and said with urgency, "If you've got an alarm signal, you'd better sound it. This boat's about to be boarded by river pirates!"

"Are you sure about that?" the pilot asked.

"There's a small boat loaded with armed men just a few feet away from the side," Ki replied. "They'll be coming aboard within the next minute or two."

Ki's tone of voice apparently convinced the pilot. He yanked at a lanyard that hung from the ceiling, and the steamboat's hoarse whistle sounded in three quick blasts followed by two longer ones. Almost at once the faint sounds of men's shouting voices came from the main deck. Ki turned to go.

"Wait a minute!" the pilot said. "You'd better stay here where you'll be safe. Those river pirates are a bad lot. They shoot to kill anybody who gets in their way!"

"I've been shot at before," Ki replied over his shoulder. "And your crew's going to need all the help it can get to fight off the pirates!"

Before the pilot could reply, the sound of a shot, and then another, rang out from the decks below. The shooting galvanized Ki into action. He ran for the stairs down to the second deck; as he did so, he reached into one of the many pockets of his well-worn black leather vest, and palmed several of the razor-edged *shuriken* secreted there. Sprinting down the passageway of the second deck, he stopped in front of Jessie's cabin door.

"Jessie?" he called.

"Ki?" she replied. Then she opened the door and stepped out, her Colt in her hand. "I was sure I heard shooting, Ki. What's happening?"

"River pirates," Ki said tersely. "I saw their boat from the top deck. They'll be aboard in a few minutes, and I suppose it's our fight as much as it is the crew's."

"How many are there?" Jessie asked.

"I didn't count, but I'd guess there are about fifteen men in the pirates' boat. I don't know how many men are in the crew, or whether they're disciplined enough to fight them off."

"Let's go help them, then," Jessie said.

Ki knew Jessie well enough to realize there was no point in suggesting that she stay in her cabin. He turned toward the stairs leading to the main deck, and she caught up with him in two quick steps. They were still a dozen yards from the stairway when two roughly dressed men carrying shotguns appeared at its head. They could not walk abreast on the narrow stairway; one of them was a step below the other.

"Take the second one," Jessie said instantly, bringing up her Colt.

Ki had a *shuriken* ready in his hand. The star-shaped blade spun glittering through the air and was halfway to its target before either of the pirates could bring up his weapon.

Jessie's shot rang out a second or less after Ki had spun

the blade, but the bullet reached its target before the *shuriken* did. The pirate at whom she's aimed was tossed back against the stair railing by the impact of the .38-caliber slug. He stayed erect for a moment, a look of surprise beginning to form on his features, then toppled slowly backward.

Ki's *shuriken* had also gone true to its mark. Before the man in the lead started to fall, the six-pointed blade had whirred past him. It buried itself in the other pirate's throat, its points severing both his jugular vein and his windpipe.

For a moment the pirate stood balanced on the stairway. His mouth began moving, but no sound came from it. Then a spurt of bright blood from the severed vessel burst in a miniature gusher that drenched his chin and one side of his face. He started to collapse, the shotgun falling from his nerveless hands and bouncing down the stairs with a clatter.

Shots and shouts from the main deck were filling the air by now. Jessie looked at the two sprawled bodies that effectively blocked the stairway for immediate use and said, "Let's go down on the other side, Ki. Maybe the stairway there is clear."

"Good. That's where their boat is," Ki told her. "The crew seems to be putting up a good fight, judging by the shooting. We might catch the pirates trying to get off."

They hurried around the stern to the opposite side of the *Northern Queen*. The stairway there was clear, and several of the stateroom doors stood ajar, indicating that the passengers had fled to one of the other decks.

"Down, I think," Jessie said.

"No, Jessie!" Ki replied quickly. "The pilot house is on the deck above. If I were a pirate trying to capture a boat, that would be my first target."

"Of course!" Jessie agreed. "You know the way, Ki. Go on, I'll be right behind you."

52

Ki took the steep, narrow stairway two steps at a time. A shot rang out from the shattered rear window of the pilot house just as his head cleared the rail, and he dropped flat, calling a warning to Jessie as he went down. He glanced back and saw that she'd stopped well below the danger level.

Reassured, Ki began crawling forward along the narrow walkway. The hump of the deck on the ship's side and the ornate railing on the outside made it impossible for him to scan the area, while the curve of the vessel toward the prow hid what lay beyond. Holding a *shuriken* ready in his hand, Ki belly-crawled ahead along the narrow walkway.

Two shots sounded just as he began his serpentine approach. One shot was from a handgun, the other from a shotgun, and they forewarned Kit that a duel for possession of the pilot house was taking place only a few yards away. He inched along until he could see the back of one of the pirates, who was crouched with two others below the hump of the top deck, trading shots with the pilot and steersman.

Without turning his head, Ki motioned with one hand for Jessie to hold her position. His other hand held a *shuriken* that he'd taken from its case while they were moving around the second deck. He saw instantly that his blade could not be effective against the two men leading the attack, and even the one in the rear was not in the best position for a *shuriken* to kill at once. He took the second-choice target that was forced on him. He whirled the blade and reached the third man, biting into the base of his skull. He yowled with pain and rose from his crouch. A rifle barked in the wheelhouse and he fell.

In reflex action on hearing the wounded man's cry of pain, his two companions turned, half-rising from their crouch. Behind him, Ki heard the sharp, familiar blast of Jessie's Colt, while at almost the same time the high-pitched crack of a rifle and the deeper, throaty boom of a shotgun sounded from the wheelhouse. Both of the pirates crumpled and lay still.

Shots were still sounding from the main deck. There was no need for Jessie and Ki to speak; they'd fought side by side in so many battles that each of them knew what to do and how the other would react.

Jessie, standing at the top of the stairway, turned and started for the lower deck. Ki was only a step or two behind her. They passed the top deck, which was deserted now, all the stateroom doors tightly closed, and descended to the next. The firing on the main deck was beginning to slacken, and between the occasional crackling of gunfire they could hear excited shouts and cries, interspersed with a few screams of pain.

"Hurry, Ki!" Jessie urged, looking over her shoulder. "If we get down there quickly, we might tip the balance against the pirates!"

Jessie got to the stairway before Ki did, and started down to the main deck. Ki had just reached the head of the stairs when he heard a woman's muffled scream coming from one of the nearby cabins. There was no way for him to identify the cabin from which the scream had come; the doors to all of them were closed. Ki began opening the doors at random, finding more than a few of them locked.

He heard the scream once more, farther away this time, and turned, returning past the stairway where he'd been standing when he heard the first cries. Now the screams were louder, and after trying three or four locked doors Ki found one that opened, and pulled it wide. Within the tiny cabin one of the pirates, a hulking giant of a man, was holding a woman down on the bunk, tearing at her clothing.

Ki attacked the big pirate from behind with a hammer-fist chop, but the man's position, bending forward, made the smashing blow ineffectual. Ki's fist fell short of reaching the pirate's neck, where it would have cracked the man's vertabrae. Instead, the blow landed high on the muscular hump of the giant's shoulders. It stung, however, and the big man reared up and turned to face Ki.

His move gave Ki a better choice. He thrust his right hand forward in a spear-hand jab that sent his stiffened fingers into the big pirate's eyes. Blinded at least temporarily, the giant flailed wildly with his fists in Ki's direction.

Even great skill such as Ki possessed could not avail against the tremendous power the giant unleashed in such a random flailing of hugely muscled arms and hamlike hands. One of the big man's wildly unpredictable blows knocked Ki's defending arm aside and landed on his head. Ki fell, and the pirate, his vision partly restored, grabbed up the fright-frozen woman and ran out the door.

Ki was not hurt when he fell. He rolled to his feet in a single fluid motion and started chasing the giant pirate, who was carrying the woman across his shoulder as though she weighed nothing at all. The shooting from the main deck was now a matter of single shots with long periods of silence between them.

Ki glanced over the rail as he ran after the pirate, who was making for the stairway to the upper deck. The pirates who had survived the boat crew's unexpectedly quick defense were piling into their boat, some of them dragging a leg or holding a hand over a bleeding wound. The outnumbered crew had suffered too, and only three or four of them were still in the fight.

After his quick glance below, Ki concentrated on catching up with the pirate. Still carrying the woman over his massive shoulder, the big man was starting up the stairway to the top deck. Ki fingered a *shuriken* as he made his way along the deck toward the stairs, but could not use the throwing blade because of the danger that his quarry might move in an unexpected direction and the razor-sharp weapon might hit the woman passenger.

From the main deck, a shotgun roared, and then Ki recognized the flat crack of Jessie's Colt; the individualized revolver had its own characteristic report, which no other gun matched. Knowing that Jessie was still safe and fighting beside the crew relieved Ki's mind, and he turned his full attention to chasing down his quarry.

Gaining the top deck, he saw that the pirate had turned and was running toward the steamboat's stern. The woman was still draped over his shoulder and still struggled ineffectually to break free.

As Ki ran along the narrow gangway in pursuit, he glanced down and saw the pirates scrambling to get into their boat. Some of them were wounded and being helped by their fellows; one or two did not wait to slide down the rope mooring the pirate craft to the *Northern Queen*, but jumped into the small, rocking vessel.

Ahead, the giant carrying the woman reached the stern. He looked and saw Ki gaining on him, then looked down at the water. The *Northern Queen* had lost way while its crew fought off the attackers, and its wheel was barely turning, holding it in midstream, letting the current carry it forward. For a moment the pirate hesitated. Then, as Ki drew closer, he straddled the rail a few feet behind the wheel housing and jumped into the water, his captive still clasped firmly in his huge arms.

Ki did not hesitate. He vaulted the low railing and dived.

Chapter 6

As Ki hit the water he arched his back, turning upward to keep his dive shallow, but the river held him in its icy grip longer than he'd thought it would. He fought his way to the surface, and when his head emerged, he treaded water until he'd recovered his breath, then peered through the darkness trying to locate the pirate and his captive.

From behind him came the splashing of oars, and when he looked around Ki saw the pirate's boat pulling away from the *Northern Queen*. The steamboat's paddlewheels were barely turning, and Ki realized that, just as he himself was doing, the big boat was drifting with the current. He scanned the surface for signs of the pirate and the woman, and just before he was ready to give up, saw two dark blobs floating on the white froth of the wake. Ki began swimming toward the figures, which he could just make out in the darkness.

He reached the first of the floating figures. It was the pirate, and Ki quickly discovered that even the man's great strength had been no match for the steam-driven wheel. Somehow he'd been caught in the spokes or paddles. His head was crushed, and he was no longer a man, but an inert hunk of flesh. Ki pushed the body away and swam toward the woman.

She was alive, but barely breathing. Ki could tell that unless he took drastic measures, she would not last even the few minutes that would be needed to get her onto the steamboat. Her breathing was shallow, and an ominous gurgling accompanied each breath.

Ki wrapped his strong arms around her and held her tightly against his chest. Each time she exhaled he tightened his embrace, squeezing hard, forcing a trickle of water from her lips with the pressure of his hugs. After a few moments of unceasing effort, the woman coughed and gasped. Suddenly she began breathing, though in a rough and broken rhythm, and struggled to free herself.

"Keep still!" Ki commanded, not knowing whether she'd regained consciousness, or could hear him. She tried to speak, but the sound was only a gurgle in her throat, and Ki repeated his command.

This time he was sure she heard him. She quit struggling, and after a few more minutes, while he continued to aid her in exhaling, she began breathing in a more normal rhythm. Ki relaxed his hold and said, "Don't try to swim. Just hold still, and I'll get you back on the boat."

Swimming on his side, one arm holding the woman's inert form, Ki started for the steamboat. The *Northern Queen* was still floating with the current, its paddlewheels now motionless. More lights were showing on the vessel, lanterns and torches as well as a pair of brilliant carbide searchlights mounted on the bow, which had been reversed to bathe the boat and the water around it in a pool of brightness.

Ki tried to see past the lighted area, but now his eyes could no longer penetrate the night's gloom. The pirate craft was hidden in the darkness beyond the glow. He neared the steamboat and began calling as soon as he was close enough for his shouts to reach the vessel. He called repeatedly before he got an answer from one of the hands on the main deck.

"Where in hell are you?" the man called. "I can hear you, but I can't see you!"

"Right behind the boat!" Ki called. "Swimming."

"I see you now," the hand called after a moment. "Just stay right where you're at. Fast as I can bend on a bollard, I'll toss you a line."

When the weighted rope sailed over his head, Ki was ready. It fell to one side, and he swam quickly to grab it. The woman was breathing more regularly now, though she still coughed and spat water each time she exhaled, and had not yet spoken. Holding the rope with a firm grip of his free hand, grasping the groggy woman in a tight embrace, Ki was hoisted to the steamboat's deck.

Jessie was among the group that had gathered to watch the rescue. She pushed her way to Ki's side and asked, "Are you all right, Ki?"

"Oh, I'm as good as ever," he assured her. "Wet and cold, but that's all. I think the lady here is all right too."

"Who is she?" Jessie asked.

"I don't know. A passenger, that's all. I happened to hear her screaming for help and got to her cabin in time to keep one of the pirates from raping her. He was a big fellow, and fought hard enough to land all three of us in the river."

"Did you have to kill him?"

"No. One of the paddlewheels did that. Then I saw the woman in the water and swam with her to the ship. How about you, Jessie?"

"I'm fine. Not a scratch."

"What about Standing Bear?" Ki asked.

"I don't know. I haven't seen him, but everything's been really confused."

A man wearing a white jacket pushed through the crowd of passengers that had gathered around Jessie and Ki and the half-conscious woman.

"Is this the passenger who almost drowned?" he asked Jessie.

"Yes. Why?"

"I'm Morrison, the chief steward. It's my job to take care of passengers who are sick or hurt or need special attention. Sorry it took me so long to get here." He looked at Ki. "You, sir? Are you the other passenger who fell overboard?"

"Yes," Ki replied. "Unless there were more than two of us in the water. But I didn't fall. I jumped in after the lady and the pirate who was trying to carry her off with him. And I'm all right, I don't need any care."

"Then I'll take the lady and see that she's looked after," the steward said. "And I'm sure the captain will want to have a word with you later, when things settle down."

"Whenever he wants to," Ki said. "By the way, Morrison, have you seen the man traveling with Miss Starbuck and me? He's an Indian, Standing Bear."

"Of course. You'll find him in the dining salon. He got a knock on the head during the fighting, but he's not really hurt. If you'd like to see him you can come along with me. That's where I'll be taking this lady."

Jessie said, "Of course we want to see him! You're sure he's all right?"

"Quite all right, ma'am. He just has a knot on his head," Morrison replied.

"Let's go, then," Ki told the steward. "Here. I'll help you with the lady. Do you know who she is, by the way?"

"Her name is Young, Mrs. C.E. Young. Her destination is Winnipeg, but beyond that, sir—"

"I don't need to know anything more," Ki said. "Come on, Morrison, let's get started. Mrs. Young does need some care, she still isn't completely conscious."

Ki and the steward lifted the woman and made a hand-cradle to carry her the short distance to the dining salon. Jessie followed them. There were ten or a dozen passengers in the big bare room, but only three or four seemed to be suffering from anything worse than slight scratches or bruises. Standing Bear saw Ki and Jessie and made his way to where they stood.

"I do not need to be here," he told them. "This"—he indicated a scratch on his forehead—"this I got when one of the pirates hit me with the barrel of a rifle, and the front sight cut me a bit. May I go with you when you leave?"

"Of course," Jessie assured him. "But I don't think they'd keep you here very long. There doesn't seem to be a doctor, but aside from the woman Ki helped out of the river, nobody looks to be very badly hurt."

"All I need is sleep," Ki said. "Everybody on board's going to be hashing over what happened until we go ashore at Winnipeg. I don't feel very talkative right now, so if you don't mind, Jessie, I'm going to my cabin and to bed."

Late the following day, Ki stood on the after deck of the *Northern Queen,* watching the red glow of sunset on the river's surface. Following a morning when everyone on board wanted to talk about the pirate attack, the subject had worn thin, and things aboard the vessel had returned to normal.

Jessie had decided to go to her cabin early. Standing Bear stood at the rail a yard away from Ki, an abstracted expression on his face as he looked at the riverbanks slipping past. They were out of the long-settled farmlands now, passing through land that was a patchwork: part farms, part untouched forest.

Footsteps tapping on the deck behind him drew Ki's attention from the shore. He turned and saw a young woman coming toward him. She stopped and asked in an uncertain voice, "Pardon me, but isn't your name Ki?"

For a moment Ki looked at the woman without recognizing her. She was not as young as she'd seemed at a distance, and with a sudden shock he realized that she was the one he'd saved from the giant pirate the day before.

She looked totally different from the bedraggled, half-conscious woman he remembered. Though mature, she had an air of youthfulness. Her features were regular, but not exceptional, not beautiful; they were simply clean-cut and pleasing. Her face bore signs of maturity but not age, and if there was any gray in the long blond hair that fell in a golden cascade down her back he could not see it. However, her eyes worried Ki. They were large and clear and deep blue, but a tiny net of almost invisible wrinkles at their corners gave her face a haunted look.

He said, "Yes. I'm Ki."

"Oh, I'm so glad I found you, Mr. Ki!" she told him. "I think you just recognized me. I'm Marian Young. You got me away from that beastly pirate and then saved me from drowning."

"You do look different," Ki said.

"Better, I hope. I was shocked when I saw myself in the mirror after I got back to my cabin," she went on. "But the steward advised me to stay in bed, and I didn't feel like getting up, or I'd have looked for you last night."

Ki sensed that she was having trouble getting to the point, and tried to make it easier for her to talk. "I stayed in my cabin, too, so you wouldn't have found me. But I'm glad to see that you've recovered. You have, haven't you?"

"Oh yes. And I wanted to find you and thank you for what you did for a perfect stranger, Mr. Ki."

"Just plain Ki, please," Ki said. "No 'mister' or any other title."

"Really? Is that all you're ever called?"

"It's what I prefer to be called, Mrs. Young," he replied. "And I didn't do anything unusual. Anybody would have helped you, under the circumstances."

"Just the same, I owe you a great deal," she went on. "I know that money can't repay you, but"—she opened her purse and took out an envelope—"I want to give you something a little more substantial than words."

Ki shook his head. "Please don't offer me anything, Mrs. Young. You don't owe me a reward. I didn't expect one, and with all apologies, I don't want one."

"But I want you to have this check," she insisted. "Surely Miss Starbuck doesn't pay you so much that you can't use some extra cash."

Ki found himself at a loss, as he always did when trying to explain his relationship with Jessie. After a long pause he said, "I don't think Miss Starbuck would approve if I let you give me a reward, Mrs. Young. Please do me a favor and don't press me to accept."

"Well..." Mrs. Young hesitated, a puzzled frown on her face, then said, "Very well. But you must know how grateful I am to you, Ki."

"That's reward enough, Mrs. Young. I hope you recover very quickly from that unhappy experience yesterday."

"I'm sure I will, Ki, and thank you again for what you did," she said. "I hope we'll find time to talk again before the boat docks at Winnipeg tomorrow night."

For a moment Ki watched Mrs. Young as she moved away, her blond hair rippling in the light breeze. Then he turned back to his contemplation of the riverbank.

"She feels you own her life now, Ki," Standing Bear said suddenly. "When she offered you money, it was to buy it back."

For a moment Ki did not understand the Ojibway's meaning, but then Standing Bear went on, "My people have a saying that when a life is saved it belongs to the one who saves it, until he gives it back to the person he saved."

"I don't feel that I own her life, Standing Bear."

"No, but *she* does."

"If she does, she'll forget about it after a while."

"Perhaps. But that is a problem for her to solve." When Ki made no reply, Standing Bear turned away from the rail and said, "I think I will go to bed now, Ki. It is too dark to see more, and we will have a long day tomorrow, when we get to Winnipeg."

There was no music in the dining salon that night, and only a few of the passengers were moving around the boat or sitting in the main salon. Ki decided to follow the example of Jessie and Standing Bear, and go to bed early.

In his cabin he did not bother to light the lamp that hung in a swivel bracket on the wall by the narrow dresser. He slipped off his black leather vest and the loose, white cotton blouse beneath it. Stepping from his rope-soled sandals, Ki let his trousers slide to the floor and tugged at the knot that held the narrow sash which looped around his waist, dropped to pass under his crotch, and then circled his waist again. Naked, he stretched a few times to relax his muscles, then lay down on the bed, cleared his mind of the day's memories, and within a few moments was asleep.

Ki's mental clock was almost unfailingly accurate. He knew that he'd slept less than an hour when the whisper of metal scraping metal brought him wide awake. He lay motionless, expecting the intruder to attack. Ki needed no preparation to reach the peak of his skill; the skill was part of him, as ready to use as his hands. He did not move, but waited to see who would come seeking him in the darkness.

When the door opened, Ki saw a shadowy figure slip through, a vague form that he glimpsed for a few seconds in silhouette against the night sky. His look was too brief for him to make out anything more than a flicker of movement as the midnight visitor entered. The door clicked shut at once, plunging the cabin into total darkness again. Ki lifted himself silently from his bed, and his bare feet made no sound as he stepped to the center of the room. Then everything became clear when he heard a whisper in the dark silence.

"Ki?"

It was a woman's voice, and Ki realized at once that Standing Bear's wisdom had been greater than he'd credited. The voice was that of Marian Young.

"Ki?" she repeated, her whisper louder this time.

"I'm here, Mrs. Young," he replied in a voice only a little louder than hers.

"Please don't be angry, Ki," she said. "I couldn't sleep for thinking of you, so I found the steward and bribed him to lend me his passkey."

"All you had to do was knock," Ki told her. "I would have opened the door."

"I couldn't be sure of that," she replied. "And I'm so lonely, Ki! I've been alone since my husband died three years ago. I know you didn't invite me, but won't you please let me stay here with you for a while?"

Ki could tell from her voice that she'd located him when he replied, and was moving closer to him while she spoke. He was prepared to feel her fingers on his bare chest, but had not expected the sharp inhalation that followed the touch of her hand on his skin. He covered her hand with his, and she gasped again as she clasped his hand and moved it to her breasts.

"Are you sure you want to stay?" he asked gently.

"If I hadn't been sure, I wouldn't have come here at all," she replied. Her free hand was stroking Ki's side now, running caressingly along his ribs, down to his hips. "But since I talked with you, I haven't been able to think of anything except..."

She stopped talking as her hand reached Ki's crotch. She cupped his sex in her soft palm, and he could feel her body begin to tremble as the tempo of her breathing increased.

"I want what I'm holding, Ki," she whispered. "But I want more than that, too. I want to be with somebody who thinks of me as myself, not just someone who says hello when I pass by. I've been without a man too long, Ki. Can't you feel how much I need you and want you?"

He said, "You didn't just come here because you felt you owed me something? You don't expect to pay me by asking me to go to bed with you?"

"No!" she said sharply. "I came to you because I thought you might have some sympathy for a lonely woman who needs a man. Not just any man, but a man who attracts her. Now, have I found the man I'm looking for, or shall I go?"

"You won't have to go, Mrs. Young."

"Marian," she broke in quickly.

"A man can get lonely, too," Ki said, his voice soft now. "And he needs a woman who feels drawn to him. Honor me by staying with me tonight, Marian."

Ki bent to kiss her, and as their lips met and their tongues entwined, Marian began stroking him gently. She gasped as she felt him swelling, and released him long enough to shrug her thin wrap off her shoulders.

Marian gasped and began to shudder gently. She pulled him closer and trapped his rigid shaft between their bodies, then began swinging her hips from side to side while her lips again sought his. Ki prolonged the embrace until Marian's movements increased in intensity, then he lifted her and stepped to the bed, where he lowered her gently and lay down beside her.

"Ki," she whispered, "it's been such a long time since

I've been with a man that I'm beginning to be afraid. Don't let me be, please. Even if I ask you to stop, don't do it."

"It's too late to stop now," Ki told her. "But don't worry, I'm not going to hurt you."

"You're so big," she replied. "Bigger than—well, bigger than I thought a man could be."

Ki did not stop to reassure her this time. He knelt above her and began caressing her nipples with his tongue, then slowly moved down her body with his caresses until his face was buried in her downy pubic hair, and her hips were rising and falling involuntarily in a steadily quickening rhythm.

"Oh, Ki!" she moaned. "You're making me feel like I never have before, even when . . . oh, I don't want you to stop, and I want to feel you inside me, but you're so big and hard that I'm afraid you'll hurt me."

Ki straightened up and said, "You'll lose your fear if you are the one in control, Marian." He lay down on the bed and lifted her above him. "Now mount me and ride in any way that gives you pleasure."

Marian hesitated for only a moment. Then she grasped Ki's rigid shaft, guided it into position, and brought her hips down with careful deliberation. Ki felt her warmth engulfing him, and resisted his urge to thrust upward. He lay quietly, his fingers caressing her breasts while she timidly lowered her body a bit further.

"It doesn't hurt at all," she whispered, surprise in her voice. "It feels wonderful."

"And it will feel better as you take me deeper," Ki promised.

"Oh yes!" she exclaimed. "And I'm not afraid now!"

She lifted her torso erect and dropped heavily on his hips. He thrust up gently, and she uttered a small shriek of delight. Then she exploded in a frenzy of activity, raising and lowering her hips in a twisting motion that brought gasps of pleasure from her throat.

"It's wonderful!" she said happily. "I didn't think I'd ever feel this good again! Stay with me now, while I—oh, Ki! Help me take you deeper! I'm—I'm—oh yes, now, Ki!"

Her body was taut under Ki's hands, her head thrown back. Small screams of delight flowed from her lips as she rocked back and forth on Ki's muscular thighs. He clasped her hips and pulled her close, thrusting upward in a single lunge and holding their bodies glued together.

Marian began twisting her hips in response to his upward movements, then suddenly she began trembling, her body writhing, and the small screams merged into a continuous cry of pleasure. Ki raised his hips for a still deeper penetration and held her close while her quivering spasms rippled to an end, and she sighed and her taut muscles went limp.

She lay in silence for a few minutes, then whispered, "Oh, thank you, Ki! I've never felt so filled and satisfied! Don't leave me, please. Not for a long time!"

"Don't worry," Ki assured her. He wrapped his arms around her and held her to him while he reversed their positions without breaking the bond of flesh that held them together. He began a slow stroking, raising and lowering his hips with long, deliberate thrusts. "We have the rest of the night ahead, and the day as well, if you wish."

"Right now I have only one wish," she sighed. "And that's for you to keep doing exactly what you're doing now. Don't stop, Ki. I've got so much lost time to make up for that I won't care if you never quit!"

★
Chapter 7

"We'll have to stay here for a couple of days," Jessie told Ki and Standing Bear as they stood on the main deck of the *Northern Queen*, waiting for the roustabouts on the dock to secure the gangplank. "The *Queen* goes on upriver to the head of navigation, and there won't be another passenger boat until the day after tomorrow."

"If you wish to hurry, we can hire horses and go at once," Standing Bear suggested.

"I don't think one day will make that much difference," Jessie replied. "And I don't know how long it will take me to find out a few things I'm curious about."

"These are the things you wanted to know that I could not tell you?" the Ojibway asked.

Jessie nodded. "It's too soon to be sure, but what you said about the land-grabbers gave me the idea that there's more behind their moves than your people suspect. If I'm right, I'm sure I can find out here in Winnipeg."

"I have cousins here, and totem brothers too," Standing Bear said. "How can I help you, Jessie?"

"Let me see what I can learn first," she suggested. "I've found that banks can provide me with just about any information I need about an area. I'll talk to the manager of my own bank's correspondent the first thing in the morning.

Then, if I'm still not satisfied, we'll call on your relatives and friends for help."

"We will be welcome to stay with them while we wait, if you like," Standing Bear went on. "I can arrange this thing very quickly."

"Oh no. That would be imposing on them. We'll go to a hotel. I'm sure there are some good ones here," she said.

"But you do not mind if I stay with my cousins?"

"Of course not. I'm sure they'd want you to."

Standing Bear nodded. "Then it is arranged. And if you wish me to help—"

"Don't worry, I'll ask you," Jessie promised.

A uniformed doorman was just emerging from the door of the Royal Bank of Manitoba to begin his day's stint when Jessie and Ki got out of the hackney cab. They felt at ease and refreshed after a night in beds that did not sway in the river's current or tremble when the paddlewheels sped up, improved as well by hot baths and a change from their traveling clothes.

"If I didn't know we were in Canada, I'd say we were in London," Ki said under his breath to Jessie as they mounted the wide stone steps to the door. "Cut stone and uniformed doormen seem to be a British custom."

Both the doorman and the building fitted the description Ki had applied to them. The doorman stood a good six feet tall, and seemed taller because of his military stance. The building was three stories tall, its gray cut stone set off by bronze-framed windows and a chased-bronze double door. It faced Portage Avenue a short distance from Main Street, at the heart of the city. As they reached the door, Jessie asked the resplendently uniformed guardian where they would find the bank's managing director.

"That would be Lord Brereton, ma'am," the doorman

replied. "Might I ask if His Lordship is expecting you?"

"He isn't, but I'm sure he'll receive me. I'm Jessica Starbuck, and I was directed to this bank by the president of the Harris Bank in Chicago." She reached into her drawstring purse and withdrew one of her business cards, which she presented to the man.

"Indeed, ma'am. I'll call a page to escort you to the director's office."

After the imperturbable doorman, Jessie was surprised when Lord Brereton appeared at the door of his private office as soon as the messenger took her card in.

Brereton was even more imposing than the doorman. He followed the prototype established in London's Threadneedle Street: tall and ruddy-cheeked, he had a clipped white mustache and wore a stiff collar above a subdued gray cravat accented with a pearl stickpin. His black morning coat was the unmistakable work of a bespoke tailor, as were his fawn-colored waistcoat and matching trousers. All that he lacked to make him a twin to the bankers Jessie had seen in London was a monocle.

"Miss Starbuck," he said with a military bow. "I was expecting you, though not as soon as this, after your man in Chicago sent me a telegram saying you might visit us. Do come in and sit down." As he spoke the invitation, Brereton looked at Ki with a question in his eyes.

For this visit, Ki had changed into more formal attire than was his usual custom. He wore a dark brown business suit and low-topped black Wellington boots. If anything, however, this attire only served to accentuate the striking Oriental cast of his features, and heightened the air of mystery that always surrounded him.

"This is Ki, Lord Brereton," Jessie said quickly. "He was my father's trusted friend, just as he is mine."

"Ah. Ki, you will be joining us, of course," Brereton

nodded. He stepped aside, showed Jessie and Ki to chairs, and settled into his own chair behind an imposing mahogany desk. "Now. How may we be of service?"

"Not financially, I'm afraid," Jessie replied.

"That's of no importance, my dear Miss Starbuck. Let's say that through you we are thanking your father for the benefits he brought to our province in the past."

"I didn't realize that Alex had done a great deal this far east in Canada," Jessie said. "Most of his interest was in the West and on the Pacific Coast."

"In his later years, of course," Brereton replied. "But he was active enough in this part of Canada during the early days of his career for a town to be given his name."

"Really?" Jessie said with genuine surprise. "I didn't know that."

"Ah, that's because you don't visit us often enough. You might want to see the town of Starbuck while you're here. It's just a few miles south of Winnipeg. If you wish to pay it a visit, it would be my pleasure to accompany you."

"Perhaps we can do that later," Jessie told the banker. "I don't know how long it will take to wind up the business that Ki and I must attend to. But thank you for the invitation."

"I'm only sorry you can't accept, but as you say, business must come first. Please tell me what I can do to help you."

"I hope you can give me some information, Lord Brereton."

"Investments, I presume?"

Jessie nodded. "Perhaps. That will depend on what I can find out about an area to the north of Winnipeg. The place is on the Winnipeg River, south of the lake about eight miles."

"If I remember correctly, that's where a large number of the Ojibway have farms," Brereton said. "What do you wish to know about it, Miss Starbuck?"

"General information, for the most part. What sort of income the present owners have been getting, prices per acre for developed and raw land, if there have been any exceptionally large farms sold lately, who bought them, if they were bought for cash or on mortgages. I'm sure I don't have to spell things out for a banker with your experience, Lord Brereton. Your bank must certainly have financed quite a few of the sales."

"Unfortunately we haven't. In spite of our prominence in the province, we've been overlooked by the buyers of the land you describe."

"Oh, you're familiar with the area up there, then?"

"More or less. Of course, I don't yet know the extent of your plans, or how you happened to become interested in such an out-of-the-way spot, but our attention was drawn to it by the recent activity in land sales."

"You might say that mine was too," Jessie told him. "As I'm sure you know, a large business such as the Starbuck enterprises develops its own private sources of information."

"And I'm sure yours must be excellent. I'm surprised they didn't uncover the details you've asked for."

"Only fools act on unverified information," Jessie replied coolly. "But if it's too much trouble for your people to confirm my data, I can certainly find others who will."

"Please don't be hasty, Miss Starbuck!" the banker urged. He tapped the call bell that stood on his desk. The office door opened, and a young man came in and stood wordlessly waiting orders. Brereton said, "Carter, ask Mr. Parsons and Mr. Bell to step in here for a moment." Turning back to Jessie, he went on, "They are the heads of our rural real estate and farm market departments. I'm sure they can answer your questions."

Within minutes there was a tapping at the door, and when Lord Brereton called "Come," the two men he'd sent for

73

appeared. He introduced Jessie, ignoring Ki, and then said, "Miss Starbuck has some questions to ask you about the farmlands at the south end of Lake Winnipeg. Please answer her as you would me."

Jessie's questions were pointed, and the answers she received from the bankers convinced her that her first suspicions had been correct. The farmlands mentioned by Standing Bear had indeed sold far below market prices and were financed by first-mortgage loans; there had been water diverted from downstream farms by the new owners, resulting in the water-short farms being offered at forced sales, and the activity in the area where the Ojibway had settled was the only one in which such sales had taken place.

However, when it came to determining the source of financing for the purchases and determining whether the buyers were in fact the actual owners, the executives summoned by Brereton confessed that they had no knowledge of such matters.

"Then send me Mitchell," Brereton ordered. "He'll know."

Mitchell arrived, and when Brereton posed the question, he pursed his lips sourly. "We weren't asked to provide financing for the transactions in question," he said. "The money came from the Wohlbehaltenhaus Leuten, in Germany."

Jessie's memory was stirred, and she asked, "Would that bank be in the Rhineland, perhaps?"

"Now that you mention it, Miss Starbuck, I believe it is," Mitchell replied. "I thought it odd at the time that an obscure provincial bank in Germany should be advancing the funds for a group from the States to buy land in Canada."

"Did you try to find out why?" Jessie pressed.

"No, Miss Starbuck. The transaction had been completed; it would have been to no purpose."

"I don't suppose you know the names of any officials of this German bank?" Jessie asked.

"I'm afraid not. It's really not in our sphere, you see." Mitchell paused thoughtfully, then added, "But a new man has just joined my department who might know." Turning to Brereton, he went on, "Young Aschenhausen. He's quite familiar with German banking and bankers."

"Send him in, then!" Brereton said. "Miss Starbuck will think we're a group of incompetents if we can't answer her questions fully!"

Aschenhausen arrived in due time. In contrast to Brereton and the others whom Jessie had seen, he was a young man. He had a Prussian accent and haircut to match it, a stiff brush of wiry blond hair only an inch or so long above his brow, the remainder of his head nearly shaved clean. He bore himself with the deportment of an army officer, stiff and unable to relax, and when introduced to Jessie, he clicked his heels and bowed over her hand, stopping before his lips touched it.

"Count von Aschenhausen has just joined our staff from the Credit Occidental," Brereton told Jessie. "He may be able to give you the information you're after."

"I'm very curious to know whether there is a Baron Ernst Josef Dolch on the board of directors of the bank in Germany that is financing the purchase of farmland around Lake Winnipeg," Jessie said. Then she added, "Or it may be that the baron holds a substantial amount of stock in the bank."

Frowning, Aschenhausen shook his head. "Of my personal knowledge, I cannot say, Fräulein Starbuck."

"But can you find out?" Brereton broke in.

"Of course, sir. But it will mean sending cables to some friends in Germany," the count replied.

"Then send them!" Brereton ordered.

"Lord Brereton," Jessie broke in, "you've done more

than enough to help me in this matter. I can't ask you to go to any more trouble."

"Nonsense, ma'am!" Brereton snapped. "There's no effort we won't make to help a client, or a possible client!" He turned back to the young German. "Send your cables, ask for an answer at once. How long will it take you to get replies?"

"A few hours. Certainly by early evening."

"Then I'll stop by tomorrow morning and see if you have the information," Jessie volunteered.

"Why wait until morning?" Brereton asked. He turned to Aschenhausen. "You can deliver the reply to Miss Starbuck at her hotel this evening, I hope?"

"Of course, if you wish."

Brereton asked Jessie, "Will you be at your hotel this evening to get the message?"

"If you insist on delivering it, of course."

"Good. I'm sure the count will see to it, then."

"To be sure." Aschenhausen's reply was accompanied by another stiff half-bow. "Miss Starbuck, it will be my pleasure to wait upon you at your hotel this evening. May I ask where you are staying?"

"At the Regal Arms. And I have no plans to go out, so any time that's convenient for you will suit me."

As soon as the young German had left, Jessie rose. "We've taken far too much of your morning, I'm afraid, Lord Brereton. I'm very grateful to you for your help, of course."

"It has been my pleasure, Miss Starbuck. And remember, if you should decide to visit the town that bears your father's name, I would be happy to escort you."

"I won't forget," Jessie promised.

As Jessie and Ki left the bank, she asked, "Did you get the same impression that I did, Ki?"

"I got a distinct feeling that His Lordship would like very much to get some business from the Starbuck companies."

"Oh that. Of course he would. But I'm involved in enough banks now, and I certainly don't need one in Winnipeg. That's not what I was talking about. I was thinking of the pattern that the land-grabbing seems to be showing."

"It shows that crooks are at work," Ki said.

"Not ordinary crooks, though. It's the same pattern we've seen so many times before."

"You mean the cartel pattern?"

Jessie nodded. "That's what set Alex against them in the first place. That's why they killed him, because they could see that he of all men understood best what their plans were."

"Yes, he did. But don't forget that he was also one of the few who had the courage to come out in the open and fight them."

Jessie nodded abstractedly; she'd been piecing together a number of memories of her own fights. She said, "Think of what we've run into just in the past few years, Ki. Besides trying to get the Circle Star, the cartel has tried to take over other rangeland in Mexico and the Indian Nation as well. Forest land in Oregon. Mineral claims in New Mexico and Montana and Nevada. Rich farmland in Nevada, and now in Canada."

"They've certainly been concentrating their attention on the major natural resources," Ki said, frowning. "I hadn't thought of it in those terms, but you're right, of course."

"And now they've moved into Canada," Jessie went on. "It's easy to see why they're picking farmland and rangeland as their targets, of course."

"For Europe's benefit, not ours," Ki said.

"Certainly. There's not a country in Europe that's totally self-sufficient, as we are on this side of the Atlantic. And

77

don't you see, Ki, the cartel's very careful to pick soft spots in places where the people who really own what they're after are too weak to fight them."

"Indians here, poor peons in Mexico, small farmers and silver miners in New Mexico," Ki said thoughtfully.

Jessie nodded. "Exactly. The cartel wants to use them as cheap labor to produce indispensable needs, such as food, which they can sell to European countries that are running short of natural resources."

"Funny," Ki said. "Alex told me almost the same thing when he was talking to me about the cartel just before they ordered their gunmen to murder him."

"Yes. But they were afraid of Alex, Ki. They could see that if they gave him time, he would persuade prominent people to join him and organize the country to fight back."

"That's something I've been thinking about, but I haven't gotten very far. Don't you think it's time we started getting some sort of organization going, Jessie? We've been fighting pretty much alone since Alex's death."

"I'd like nothing better, Ki. But this country—and I suppose the rest of the world as well—isn't ready yet to pay much attention to what a woman says, even one named Starbuck."

"Lord Brereton was very interested in finding out what you planned to do."

"Maybe I'm overly sensitive, but I got the feeling he was being condescending all the time he was telling me how eager he was to help."

"I wonder what he'd have done if you'd told him that your real purpose in coming here was to help the Ojibway?"

"I'm sure he'd have been equally polite, but I'm also sure he'd have been much less eager to help."

"In one way, Standing Bear's people are smarter than Lord Brereton and his kind. At least they realized there was

78

something wrong, even if they didn't know what to do about it," Ki observed.

"They knew enough to call on us for help. And we'd better begin thinking about how we can give it to them."

"How can we do that until we see the size of the problem?"

"I don't know yet. But I do know we'll find a way." Jessie was silent for a moment, then she said, "I think we'd better change our plan to take the steamboat the rest of the way, Ki. I want to get a closer look at the land and see how bad the situation really is."

"We'll be leaving earlier than we'd planned, then?"

"Yes. Let's find Standing Bear and tell him. We'll spend the afternoon buying the gear we'll need to camp out, and leave early in the morning."

Chapter 8

A messenger provided by the hotel had brought Standing Bear to the Royal Arms. He sat with Jessie and Ki in the sitting room of the suite Jessie had taken in anticipation of a longer stay.

"How long will it take us to make the trip to your village?" Jessie asked him.

"Three days. Four, if there is rain."

"What difference does the rain make?" Ki wanted to know.

"In places along the shortest trail there is muskeg we must cross. If the rain falls, we cannot use the short trail. We will have to take a longer way, and go around the bogs."

"Then we'd better carry provisions for five days," Jessie said, making a note on the list she was preparing. "I'd rather carry a bit more than we need, and not risk running short."

Standing Bear nodded. "That is wise. Even if we take that much extra food, we will still need only one packhorse."

"If we're going to start at daylight tomorrow, we'd better go out now and buy our provisions and other gear," Ki said. He turned to Standing Bear and asked, "Are you sure your brother's son will have four horses for us?"

"He will have them," the Ojibway answered. "I will bring them myself tomorrow morning before sunrise to the hotel's stable, and wait there for you. And when I told my nephew of our trip, he offered to go with us, if you would like for him to."

"That might be a good idea," Jessie said thoughtfully. "I think we'll accept his offer, Standing Bear. Even the extra food we'll need won't make another horse necessary."

"I should go now and tell him," Standing Bear said. "He will need time to get ready, if we are leaving early tomorrow."

"What about the provisions and other gear that we have to buy?" Ki asked. "We'd better get them first."

"Suppose we do that now?" Jessie suggested. She caught Ki's eye and went on, "I'll have to hurry back here to the hotel to meet Count von Aschenhausen when he brings me the information from the bank, but you could go with Standing Bear and talk to his nephew, make sure he wants to go."

Ki caught Jessie's unspoken message. He said, "Of course. We'll take the camping gear and food with us and pack it for the trail. And I'd like to take a look at the horses too."

"You do not say this thing, but I know you also want to look at my nephew," Standing Bear said in a quiet voice. "I do not blame you for wanting to be sure of him, Ki, but you do not need to worry about Mizuan. You can trust him as I think you have come to trust me."

"I'm glad you understand," Jessie told the Ojibway. "Ki and I have learned to be very careful, especially in strange places. Now, if there's nothing more to add to the list, let's go and get our gear."

Shopping for trail equipment, even in a strange city, was no real problem for Jessie and Ki. They'd been faced with similar situations many times before, and with the aid of Standing Bear and the driver of their hack, they completed the job by midafternoon. As they came out of the last store

81

and opened the door of the boxlike hackney, Jessie looked at the heap of equipment: heavy blankets, a bucket, skillet and a stew pot, a coffeepot, utensils, extra ammunition for her Colt and Standing Bear's rifle, and food enough for their three-day trip.

"There's not really enough room for three of us in there, Ki," she said. "You and Standing Bear go ahead. I'll walk down the street toward the hotel and flag the first hack I see."

Ki looked at the light traffic on Ellice Avenue and said, "This doesn't seem to be a good time of day to find a stray hackney, Jessie. You might have to walk all the way."

"That doesn't bother me a bit. I need to exercise after those days on the steamboat. Go ahead. I'll have plenty of time to rest before supper."

Jessie watched the cab roll off, and then started walking slowly down the street. The afternoon was bright, but the air was cool and buildings shaded most of the sidewalk. She strolled along, glancing into the store windows, enjoying the feeling of being an anonymous face in a strange city.

Reaching Main Street, she turned and continued to the Royal Arms. She stopped at the desk to get the key to the suite she and Ki occupied, and the clerk handed her an envelope as well as the key. Jessie opened the envelope; it contained Count von Aschenhausen's engraved card and a note on hotel stationery telling her that he would return at a later hour with the information she had requested, followed by the count's flamboyant signature.

In her room, Jessie decided there'd be plenty of time for a leisurely bath before the count returned and before Ki and Standing Bear would complete their errand. She soaked in the warm water and enjoyed a half-dozing rest on the chaise lounge in her bedroom before dressing. Then she went to her portmanteau and removed from a skillfully concealed pocket in its lining a slim, leather-covered black book. It was a condensed version of a larger volume that was stored in a secret compartment in her father's rolltop desk in the study back at the Circle Star. In this ledger, Alex had kept a careful record of all the cartel operatives and business connections he'd uncovered in his many encounters with the sinister European cartel. Jessie had continued to add to and revise the information since Alex's death, and had also made this facsimile, which she kept in a sort of personal code that only she understood.

She knew that Baron Dolch's name was at the head of an impressive list of entries—not surprising, since he was the son of one of the cartel's founders—but when she now looked up his name, she found no reference to the Wohl-behaltenhaus Leuten. If he turned out to be connected in some way with the German bank, she would have to add this information to his dossier.

Then she searched through the book for a possible mention of Count Wilhelm von Aschenhausen. Nothing turned up, but of course Jessie realized this only meant that neither she nor her father had come across his name before.

She had just put the book away again when a rapping sounded on the door of the outer room. As she went to the door, she glanced in passing at the travel clock on her dressing table. Its hands indicated six o'clock. She opened the door; as she'd expected, her caller was the count.

"Good evening, *gnadige Fräulein,*" he greeted her, bowing over her extended hand. "It is a pleasure to greet you once again."

"Do come in," Jessie said. "I got the message you left on your first visit, and I'm sorry I was out when you called earlier. Ki and Standing Bear and I were buying supplies for our trip north."

"It is nothing. Do not give it another thought."

"I'm glad you came back," Jessie went on. "We've changed our plans and the three of us will be leaving for the Ojibway country in the morning. I understand that it's quite unsettled, so we're preparing to camp out."

"I know Ki, of course." The count frowned. "Standing Bear I do not recall."

"He's an Ojibway man who's—" Jessie paused momentarily before finishing, "—who's going to guide us around the area to the north, the area I was inquiring about at the bank."

Aschenhausen nodded. "The farmlands area."

After they'd settled into chairs, Jessie went on, "It's kind of you to take the trouble to help me."

"No trouble, none at all," the count replied.

"You've heard from your friend in Germany, then?"

"A cable from him arrived and I came to tell you at once. When you asked for the information regarding Baron Dolch, I had the idea that you thought it important."

"I'm very interested, of course. What did your friend in Germany find out?"

"Your intuition was quite good, Miss Starbuck. The baron is indeed a director as well as a large investor in the Wohlbehaltenhaus Leuten."

Jessie nodded slowly, turning the information over in her mind.

"You seem quite concerned, Miss Starbuck," Aschenhausen said. "Is it that you find my message to be bad news?"

"No," Jessie replied noncommittally. "I was half expecting the answer you've brought me."

"You are a remarkable lady, Miss Starbuck," the count said. "I will not, as you say in America, beat around the bush. I find you quite fascinating, a woman so young, to be managing such large affairs."

"It wasn't my choice," Jessie replied. "I'm just carrying on the work that my father started. I feel it is what he'd expect me to do."

Aschenhausen's face grew sober, and he nodded. "Ah yes. Lord Brereton told me of his tragic death, assassinated by bandits. But you give yourself too little credit, Miss Starbuck. May I speak frankly?"

"Do, by all means," Jessie replied.

"I would like to become better acquainted with you."

"I take that as a compliment," Jessie said, managing to hide her surprise at his unexpected bluntness. "But I'm—"

"Please," Aschenhausen broke in. "If you will permit me to continue." He paused, then went on, "You seem quite alone this evening, and the hour of dinner is near. Would you think I was presuming if on such short acquaintance I invited you to dine with me?"

"I don't think it's presumptuous," Jessie told the young German after a moment of thought. "But I'm expecting Ki to come back quite soon."

"Ah. The young Japanese. Your—your—how shall I say it, Miss Starbuck?"

"There's only one way to say it," Jessie replied quickly, her voice firm. "Ki is to me what he was to my father, a valued friend as well as an assistant."

"I did not assume differently, I assure you, Miss Starbuck," the count said apologetically. "But unless there is a matter of importance that forces you to wait for him, I cannot see why his absence would interfere with our dining together. If you are leaving tomorrow, you should have at least this one evening in which to relax from traveling."

Jessie had recovered from her surprise by now. On more than one occasion in the past, men whom she'd just met had prefaced an invitation to dinner with praise of her charm; she was accustomed to having men find her attractive both because of her looks and her position. She had no illusions about Aschenhausen's motives. Jessie had seen the type before, the sons of penniless aristocrats who'd come to America with the idea of peddling their titles to rich, unmarried women.

Her mental debate lasted only a few seconds before the thought occurred to her that a conversation with the count, if skillfully conducted, might yield something of interest.

"I don't suppose it's terribly important for me to talk to Ki tonight," she said, frowning thoughtfully, as though the decision were a hard one. "And he may not even be here by dinnertime. Yes, Count von Aschenhausen, I'll accept your invitation."

"Good!" the young German smiled. "I'm glad I overcame my hesitation about inviting you. I was afraid that it might not seem proper to you, and that you might think my motive was something other than the genuine admiration which so attracts me to you."

"I hope you don't have anything formal in mind," Jessie went on. "Since this is a business trip, I didn't bring any evening dresses."

"No, no," the count said quickly. "I know a small, quiet cafe where the food and service are excellent, and the patrons seldom wear formal clothing."

"What time should I be ready?" she asked.

Aschenhausen took out an ornately engraved hunter-cased watch and consulted it. "An hour? An hour and a half? Or do you prefer to dine even later?"

"Let's say an hour and a half," Jessie replied. "Will that be convenient for you?"

86

"My dear Miss Starbuck, I would make convenient any time that you set. An hour and a half, then."

Ki had not returned when Aschenhausen called for Jessie at seven-thirty. As they went through the lobby of the Royal Arms, on their way to the door, Jessie said, "I'll just step over to the desk and leave word for Ki that we're having dinner together. Then he won't be worried because I'm not in the hotel."

"Please permit me to perform that small service for you," the count said. When Jessie did not protest, he went to the desk and spoke briefly to the clerk, then returned to Jessie's side. "It is done," he told her. "Now we can enjoy our dinner without any cares."

A hackney cab was waiting outside the hotel door, and the count handed Jessie in, then took his place beside her. He did not speak to the driver, and Jessie assumed he'd already told the man what their destination was to be.

"Perhaps I should have asked if you enjoyed French cuisine before reserving a table at the restaurant where we will dine," Aschenhausen said as the hackman negotiated two curves in quick succession and the cab rumbled across the St. Mary's Street Bridge.

Jessie was looking out the window at the lights of boats on the Red River of the North. She turned back to the count and said, "I do, very much, as a change from the plain food that we eat on my ranch."

He went on, "And the cafe where we will dine is situated on a high bank near the river, so you will be able to watch the lights of the boats as we eat."

"That sounds very enjoyable, Count. I'm sure I'll like it."

"Then there is only one thing I need to begin the evening," Aschenhausen replied.

"And what is that?"

"If you could bring yourself to give up formality and use my given name."

"Wilhelm?"

"Or Willy, if you prefer."

"Of course," Jessie said. "I'll have to decide as we go along which I think suits you best."

"Thank you, Jessie. Now I feel that our evening is well started."

A few minutes later the hackman pulled up at a large red brick building that at some time in the past had obviously been a luxurious private home. The façade had no sign on it, only a small brass name plate beside the door, which Jessie could not read at a distance. Aschenhausen did not wait for the hackman to open the door, but did so himself and gave his hand to Jessie as she got out of the cab.

Inside, the appointments matched the building's unostentatious exterior. Jessie could see that three large rooms had been converted into a dining area; the wall partitions had been only partly removed to form three large alcoves, each containing two tables spaced at discreet distances. Candelabras on the walls and tables provided the lighting.

Only one table, in the first alcove, was occupied. Two men in business suits sat talking in low voices. They paid no attention to Jessie and the count as they entered, and did not look up when a small, middle-aged man wearing a waiter's white coat came to escort them to one of the tables in the rear alcove.

Aschenhausen held Jessie's chair, and when she was seated he asked, "Would you like one of your new American cocktails before dinner, Jessie?"

She shook her head. "No, thank you. I really don't drink a great deal, Willy. On the Circle Star we don't allow the cowhands to drink, and I only keep a bottle or two of brandy and whiskey, mostly for medicinal purposes."

"Surely when you travel—"

"When I travel, it's on business, and a dinner for two is a very rare occasion."

"Then I must make sure you enjoy ours a great deal," the count said. He nodded to the waiter. "You may begin serving us now, Louis."

Jessie had only enough time to glance out the window at the lights of the boats on the Red River of the North before the waiter returned with stemmed glasses and a bottle of sherry. He placed the glasses on the table and filled them, then left without speaking.

Aschenhausen picked up his glass, and when Jessie made no move to reach for hers, he said, "Surely you'll have a sip of sherry before dinner? Or perhaps you'd prefer something else, a small sip of schnapps—"

"This will do nicely," Jessie replied. She picked up her glass and sipped the sherry, but it was bitter to her taste and she set it aside quickly.

"Don't you approve of the sherry?" the count said.

"I'm sorry, but it tastes bitter to me."

"Then let me order you a light wine," he suggested. He raised his finger, and when the waiter came to the table, he said, "Louis, bring a bottle of my Moselle with the soup. The special Bernkasteler Schwanen that is in my private closet."

Several minutes passed before the waiter returned, carrying a tray on which there were small bowls of soup, a tall brown bottle, and fresh glasses. After serving the soup he opened the wine and passed the cork to the count. Aschenhausen smelled the cork and nodded. The waiter bowed and filled Jessie's glass, but when he started around the table with the bottle, the count waved him back.

"I'll finish the sherry first," he said. Then he turned to Jessie. "Sip the wine and see if you find it palatable."

Jessie took a small swallow of the pale, straw-colored wine. It was delicious, an essence of grape and sunshine. She lifted the glass for another sip, and the count smiled.

"I see it pleases you," he said.

"It's very good indeed, Willy." Jessie sipped once more before tasting her soup. The subtle flavor of the creamy soup seemed to be amplified by the lingering taste of the wine. She took another sip, then said, "I don't think I've ever tasted a wine that I like better. What did you call it? Bern—something?"

"Bernkasteler Schwanen. It is one of the finest from the Moselle region of Germany. When I drink it I feel a bit sad. It reminds me of my homeland."

"At the bank this morning, I got the impression that you came from the Rhineland," Jessie said, taking another swallow of the wine.

Aschenhausen shook his head. "No. Though the Moselle and the Rhineland are close together." He refilled Jessie's glass, which now held only a few drops in its rounded bowl. "Enjoy the wine, Jessie. I shall order another bottle when this is emptied."

Jessie lifted the glass and sipped generously. She said, "I think this is quite the nicest wine I've ever tasted. I'm almost tempted to get some for the Circle Star. Could you arrange for me to buy it, Willy?"

"Of course. It will be my pleasure."

"Then we'll see about ordering it when I get back from the Ojibway country."

"You are planning to invest in farmland there, I suppose?"

"I'm not sure. It will depend on—" Jessie stopped short, wondering why she'd been very close to revealing her plans. To cover her silence, she took another swallow of the wine. Then she said, "What I do will depend on several things."

"I was not trying to inquire into your business affairs, Jessie," the count said.

"Of course," she replied.

She looked across the table at him and shook her head. Aschenhausen seemed to be sitting in the center of a hazy outline. She lifted her eyes. The candelabras on the walls and tables were blurred, veiled by a shimmering nimbus. When she narrowed her eyes and tried to stare at the two men who sat in the front alcove, they too seemed to be wrapped in a thin fog.

"Is something wrong?" the count asked.

"No," Jessie replied, her voice uncertain. She lifted her half-emptied wineglass and drained it. The wine had warmed a bit while sitting on the table, and now it seemed bitter to her.

"Look at me, Jessie!" Aschenhausen commanded.

Jessie tilted her head back, finding it heavy and wanting nothing more than to let it loll forward. The entire restaurant was a blur now, a shimmer of light and darkness. Through it she was vaguely aware that vaguely defined forms were converging on the table where she and Auschenhausen sat.

With equal vagueness, Jessie was aware that the count was moving, though she could not see him clearly now, even at such a short distance. She tried to stand up, but the muscles in her legs did not respond. Putting her hands on the table, she began pushing against the top while commanding her legs to lift her.

For a moment Jessie's mind cleared, and she knew that something was terribly wrong. She made one final effort to stand, but it was futile. She was dimly aware of voices, but could not tell whether they were close by or distant; she heard only the sounds they made, not the words.

Then the lights and sounds vanished and Jessie dropped into a void of dark silence.

Chapter 9

Jessie felt a panic-stricken moment when she opened her eyes and saw nothing but impenetrable blackness. She opened her mouth and started to call out, but her throat was dry and scratchy, and instead of a loud cry only a harsh, rasping whisper came from her mouth. Then her panic ended as suddenly as it had come upon her, and her rigid self-control took command. After the blackness that shrouded her, the first thing of which she was really aware was a strange odor that hung in the air, but she ignored the peculiar smell in spite of its persistence.

She began flexing her hands, and their stiffness soon gave way. She dropped her hands to her sides, and when they brushed against her thighs she sat bolt upright with the astonished realization that she was totally naked.

When the shock of feeling only her bare skin subsided, Jessie first made sure that she was indeed without clothing by passing her hands quickly over her entire body. Only then did she accept the fact that she was naked, lying on a bed that gave off a pungently offensive smell. The odor seemed to hang around her in an invisible miasma, a strong, musky fragrance with a hint of human sweat.

She ran her hands over her body again, this time feeling for bruised or sore spots, but she found none. Apparently, whoever had imprisoned her in the pitch-black room had not harmed her before leaving her here. For the next few moments she lay motionless, trying to resolve the puzzle, but the drug she'd been given was still working, and her usually quick mind was not functioning with its usual speed and precision.

For a few irrational seconds Jessie thought about raising her voice and shouting. Then her common sense asserted itself once more. She relaxed and lay back quietly, ignoring the all-pervading odor of the unpleasant perfume, trying to form a plan, and decided at once that her most important job was to orient herself in her strange, invisible surroundings before she moved on to tackling the bigger problem of discovering where she was and how she'd gotten there.

In spite of her disorientation, she felt no panic. She lay motionless, her mind fully returned to alertness now, and recalled the last moments of consciousness she remembered.

There had been the restaurant and the dinner, and the German wine ordered by Count von Aschenhausen. Jessie remembered that the young count had not touched the wine, and realized immediately that he had drugged it. She remembered the shadowy forms that she'd seen approaching the table during her last few seconds of awareness, and wondered whether the other men had been hired by the count to be on hand and help him control her.

Obviously she was no longer in the restaurant. If it gave her no other clues, the strange, repulsive odor told her that. Moving with slow deliberation, Jessie swung her feet off the side of the bed and stood up. She was shaky and weak, and was forced to fight to keep her balance, but she managed to remain standing.

Winning even such a small victory encouraged her. Ignoring her nakedness, she stepped away from the bed. Belatedly she began counting her steps as she moved. She was able to take only three faltering, hesitant steps before bumping into a wall. For a moment she stood motionless, her hands exploring the wall on both sides for furniture or similar obstacles. She found nothing, and began walking slowly parallel to the wall, trailing her left hand against it as she moved and using her right hand to grope in the blackness in front of her.

She'd gone only a short distance farther when the hand that she kept pressed to the wall encountered a wooden doorframe. Jessie stopped and ran her fingertips over the door panels until she'd located the doorknob. She tried it cautiously. The knob turned easily, but when she tried to pull it toward her, the door did not move. A slow, careful push failed to budge the door in the opposite direction; it was locked.

While Jessie stood motionless, debating her next move, she heard a whisper of noise, more a suggestion than an actual sound, coming from the room into which the door opened. She pressed an ear to the nearest panel and heard the subdued rise and fall of voices in the room beyond.

After a few moments of concentration, Jessie could tell that the voices were those of both men and women, for whatever was being said brought occasional bursts of laughter, and the high-pitched female voices cut through the lower male guffaws. Between laughs, the conversation was nothing but a jumble of sound at a level too low to enable her to make out what was being said. After several minutes had passed and the voices still sounded like gibberish, Jessie gave up trying to listen and continued her exploration of the room.

She came to a corner, and kept moving along the wall until the hand with which she was groping in advance of her movement met a piece of furniture. Passing her fingers over the obstacle, she quickly determined that it was a dresser or bureau. She stepped in front of it and began exploring the surface.

Her hand encountered a cool metal cylinder that she quickly identified as a lamp base. She groped on the dresser top, feeling for matches, but found none. The only objects her fingers encountered were a small glass bottle and a comb.

Next she began opening the drawers. The small twin upper drawers held two or three more cosmetic containers, all carrying the same odor of the unpleasantly potent perfume that had flooded her nostrils when she was on the bed. The wide center drawers contained only a few rectangles of thick, soft cloth, which she identified as washcloths or small face towels.

Returning her hands to the bureau's surface, she repeated her earlier search, but it only confirmed what she'd learned the first time she'd felt over it. She lifted the bottle to her nose, almost certain that it would carry the same perfume she'd first smelled on the bed, and her suspicion proved correct. When she picked up the comb, she discovered a few long hairs and that three of its teeth had been broken off, but that was all.

Puzzled because the drawers had held no clothing, but realizing that she needed to continue her blind search of the room, Jessie dropped the comb and moved on past the dresser. She bumped into a chair that stood against the wall a short distance beyond it, and just past the chair she came to the second corner she'd encountered. A few steps farther, and she felt the framework of another door.

This time when she pressed her ear to the panels she could hear nothing. She listened for what seemed to be a long time before hearing any noise at all, then the clicking of heels on bricks gave her the clue she needed: this door opened onto a street.

Jessie was reluctant to move on. She realized that she'd have no frame of reference to use in marking the location of the door once she'd left it, but she also realized the need to learn all that she could about her surroundings. She stared along the wall beyond the door, reached the room's third corner, and before she'd taken three steps along it her exploring right hand was stopped by another piece of furniture.

Feeling its outlines, Jessie was sure that she'd come to a small washstand, and knew the bed must stand just beyond it. She groped over the little cabinet's surface and encountered the cool, slick outlines of a china washbowl. When she groped into the bowl, her fingers touched the water pitcher that stood inside it.

Suddenly Jessie was no longer able to ignore the parched, irritating dryness of her throat. She picked up the pitcher and was about to lift it to drink when the idea occurred to her that the water might be drugged. Reluctantly she replaced it in the washbowl and bent to investigate the compartment that she knew was always a feature of such pieces of furniture. A moment of groping satisfied her that the compartment contained nothing more than the customary night jar.

Moving with more confidence now, though she still could not see through the blackness, Jessie closed tbe compartment and took a step forward, certain she'd circled the room and was now very close to the bed again. She reached it on her next step, its pungent odor rising to alert her. In spite of the smell, she sat on the side of the bed while she went over the sparse list of her discoveries.

In a flash, the answer came to her. She was imprisoned in one of the rooms of a whorehouse. Strangely, she felt herself relaxing now that she'd solved the riddle of her confinement. Her quick mind projected the most probable sequence of her imprisonment. After being overcome by the drugged wine, she'd been taken to the brothel and stripped by her captors to stop her from going out on the streets if she should regain consciousness and manage to escape before they could return to deal with her. The choice of a place to hold her was no mystery; the cartel's agents operated in both the world of financial crimes and the underworld of criminal violence.

There were still many unanswered questions in Jessie's mind, the uppermost of these being how she could manage to escape before her captors returned.

Rising, she groped her way across the room and searched the dresser drawers a second time, looking for a hairpin or a discarded corset stay—anything that she might use in an effort to pick the lock on the door leading to the street. Her second search was as fruitless as her first. Leaning against the dresser, Jessie fought down her frustration and tried to think more clearly. Inspiration struck her; the bedsprings might have a loose wire that she could work free and bend into a lockpick.

Hope revived, she went back to the bed and began wrestling the heavy mattress off. She was standing with one corner of the mattress in her hands when the grating of a key sounded at the interior door. Before she could drop the mattress, the door swung open. She glimpsed a man's silhouette in the panel of light before the light striking her dilated pupils blinded her. The sudden exposure was as painful as it was surprising. Jessie instinctively closed her eyes and stood helplessly beside the bed, still holding the mattress.

When the man spoke she recognized the voice at once, and at least one of the mysteries was cleared up. The speaker was Count von Aschenhausen.

"What a becoming pose, my dear Jessie!" he said mockingly. Then his tone changed completely to one of cold menace, as he went on, "But you can open your eyes now. I want you to see the gun I'm holding, so that you will realize how foolish it would be to try to attack me and escape."

Jessie did not doubt that he was holding a gun, but she did not open her eyes at once. She said coolly, "I've been in the dark so long that I can't see right now. But I'm not going to try to run, Willy. Not now, at least."

She heard the click of the door closing and the rasp of the key turning in the lock, followed by the scratching of a match. She could see its glow through her closed eyelids, and realized that within a few moments her normal vision would return.

Aschenhausen said, "I advise you not to move, Jessie. I am going to light the lamp, then we will talk."

Jessie listened to his footsteps crossing the room, and the clinking of glass on metal as he lifted the lamp chimney. She could tell by the changed intensity of the light shining on her lids when he touched the match to the wick, for a sudden flare of brightness struck her eyes. Then, as he adjusted the lamp wick, the light settled to a steady glow. She opened her eyes now, and found that she could see without painful squinting.

Aschenhausen was turning away from the dresser. In one hand he held a nickel-plated revolver; from the lanyard loop in front of its trigger guard Jessie recognized the gun as a single-action Mauser, and judged from its size that it was the .32-caliber model. He looked at her, his round face wreathed in a gloating grin. "Capturing you will earn me a great deal of credit with my associates," he told Jessie. "You have given us much trouble, Jessica Starbuck, and because of you we have lost a great deal of money as well as some of our most valued men. Now you must repay us."

Jessie did not need the count's revealing words to know

that she'd fallen into the hands of a highly placed cartel operative. She said in a level voice, "I intend to go right on giving your despicable outfit trouble. Make no mistake about that."

"Ah, you are boasting now!" the count told her. "I enjoy nothing better than breaking the spirit of a woman such as you! When our chief arrives tomorrow, I shall ask for that pleasant job. But since you know our organization, you will understand that what happens to you eventually is not completely in my hands. I have you in my sole control only for tonight, and I have pleasant plans for ways to spend it. I advise you not to resist me, Jessie."

"I don't need to ask what your plans are," Jessie told the young German coldly. "Whether you're man enough to carry them out is something else again."

"I do not think you will choose to die tonight," he said. "But we will begin now to find out. First I must enjoy looking at you." Raising the muzzle of his pistol, he went on, "Let go of the mattress, Jessie, and stand where I can see you better."

Jessie's quick mind had been working at top speed. She knew that for the moment she was helpless, but from the instant when the German had hinted at his immediate intentions, she'd begun to think of ways to turn his plans to her advantage.

Keeping her face expressionless, she let the corner of the mattress fall and moved away from the bed. She counted on Aschenhausen's obvious admiration of her naked body to keep him from noticing that her move edged her a few feet closer to him. She was close to the center of the room now. After she'd moved, she stood quietly, her arms by her sides.

"Very beautiful," Aschenhausen said, his eyes gleaming.

"I like the way your breasts stand so erect, my dear Jessie. Later I will enjoy them even more, but first I must inspect each of your attractions more closely."

Jessie neither answered nor moved. She stared past the German's head at the wall, still keeping her face expressionless.

"Turn around slowly now," the count commanded. "I want to see you from every angle before we go further."

Obediently, Jessie began moving. She shifted her feet with slow deliberation, seeming to avoid looking at her captor when they were face to face, but actually watching him covertly. She did not expect him to relax his guard this early, but was ready to move if he did. After she'd made three complete turns, the count snapped his fingers.

"Enough of this!" he said curtly. "You will turn your back to me now, and stand without moving until I tell you what you must do next."

Jessie suppressed her desire to attack the count in spite of the revolver he was holding, and turned her back to him. She did not risk turning her head to see what he was doing when she heard soft, almost inaudible noises coming from the spot where he stood, but controlled her impatience to spring into action. She'd been standing quietly for several minutes when Aschenhausen spoke again.

"Now we will begin our little pleasures," he said.

Jessie could tell from his voice that he'd come closer to her. She felt the hard, cold muzzle of the revolver jab into her neck, and flinched in spite of her resolution to hold on to her self-control. Then Aschenhausen's free hand touched her back, high between her shoulders, and moved caressingly down to the beginning of her buttock-crease. She tightened her muscles in an involuntary reflex and heard the count chuckle.

"You are sensitive to my touch," he gloated. "That is a good sign, Jessie. It promises me much pleasure before the night is a great deal older."

Aschenhausen's free hand was fondling Jessie's buttocks now, but the hand holding the revolver remained steady. He rubbed his palm over their firmly rounded contours, then slid his hand below them. Jessie felt his fingers wriggle between her thighs, and though she tried to keep from flinching again when she felt him beginning to probe, she could not avoid an involuntary twisting of her hips in revulsion against his invading touch.

"Very sensitive indeed," he chuckled. He'd forced his fingers between the cheeks of Jessie's buttocks now, but she was prepared for his touch and remained stoically unmoving. She did not move when she felt his naked body press against her, or when she felt him thrust his erection between her thighs. It may have been her indifference to his caresses that triggered the count's anger, for suddenly his voice became cold and menacing in spite of his hand's increasingly urgent movements.

"Enough of this!" he grated. "I am ready to begin now! Bend forward! Quickly! I want you to feel me enter you! Hurry, woman! Bend, I tell you! Do not keep me waiting!"

Jessie waited for a moment, trying to sense the instant when she could no longer delay obeying, the moment when Aschenhausen's anger would exceed his caution. She moved then, spreading her feet and bowing from the waist in a single coordinated motion. The pressure of the revolver was no longer on her spine.

At the apex of her bend, when she could see the count's bare feet and legs between her own spread legs, Jessie snaked a hand back with the quickness of a striking rattlesnake. She locked her hand on Aschenhausen's ankle and jerked with all the force she could exert.

He yelled as he toppled backward, his gun dropping from his hand as his arms flailed involuntarily in a futile effort to retain his balance, but he fell heavily, landing on his back on the floor. Jessie did not make the mistake of trying to scramble for the revolver. She twirled on the ball of one foot, raising the other foot as she spun around.

Her raised foot jerked out and her heel smashed into Aschenhausen's temple. It landed squarely on the target she'd aimed at, the vulnerable spot just above his ear, between the sphenodial and temporal bones. His body quivered, then he lay still. A thin trickle of blood, only a few drops, oozed from his ear.

Jessie had brought her torso erect at the beginning of her spinning kick. She bent over Aschenhausen's body and pressed her palm flat on his chest. She did not feel a heartbeat. With a shuddering sigh, she straightened up and stood for a moment with her eyes closed until she'd regained her composure. The count was not the first dead man Jessie had seen, nor the first to meet his fate at her hands, but death from a duel with rifle or pistol came at a distance, not within an arm's length.

Her trembling lasted only a few moments. Keeping her eyes turned away from the naked body on the floor, Jessie moved at once to carry out the plan she'd conceived when she realized what her captor had planned. Setting her jaw, she dragged the body of the count to the bed and rolled it underneath, where it would be hidden from anyone who gave the room a casual glance.

She returned to the heap of the dead man's clothing that lay beside the dresser. Picking up the trousers, shirt, and coat, she slipped into the still-warm garments and slide her feet into the shoes. All the clothing was too large, but Jessie counted on the night to help her avoid being noticed, if she succeeded in getting out of the brothel.

103

She looked at the door that led outside, but had no way to open it. The key to the inner door was still in the lock, where the count had left it. Crossing the room, Jessie had started to turn the key when a thought struck her. Removing it, she went to the door that opened on the street and tried the key in it. For a moment the lock resisted, then Jessie twisted harder and it grated open.

Pausing only long enough to blow out the lamp, Jessie stepped out the door and started walking slowly through the darkness along the deserted street.

★

Chapter 10

To Jessie's relief, the street on which she found herself after escaping was totally deserted. She walked along blindly, not knowing where she was, whether she was going toward the center of town or away from it, or how far she'd have to walk before she could find out. The only thing of which she was sure was that the hour must be very late indeed, for there were almost no lights showing in the windows of the houses she passed, no carriages or wagons on the streets, and she met no pedestrians.

Thinking of her experiences of the night, Jessie decided that she had no one but herself to blame for what had happened. If her analysis of the situation that had driven Standing Bear's people to seek her help had been more thorough, she might have seen the hand of the cartel in it more clearly.

She chided herself for failing to realize from the beginning that Count von Aschenhausen was a cartel agent, and for letting her customary vigilance lapse enough to put her in such a deadly predicament. Her thoughts were broken by the soft clopping of hooves. Jessie looked toward the sound and saw the glow of a light, then a canvas-topped wagon with a lighted lantern on its seat canopy turned into the street from an intersection just ahead. The wagon went only a few yards before it began turning into another intersection.

Jessie put thinking aside and began running. The oversized shoes she was wearing slowed her down, but she got within a dozen yards of the wagon just before it completed its turn.

"Wait!" she called as loudly as she could. "Please stop for a minute! I need your help!"

For a moment she thought the driver had not heard her, then the wagon slowed and halted. Jessie caught up with it and came to a panting stop.

"What's the matter, sonny?" the driver asked as Jessie came into the edge of the dim lanternlight.

Jessie was still several paces from the wagon. She asked, "What time is it?"

"Getting on to four o'clock. I left the dairy—" The milkman got his first clear view of Jessie as she moved into the circle of light cast by the lantern. His jaw dropped as he stared at her for a moment, then blurted, "What the devil are you? A him or a her?"

Ignoring his question, Jessie said, "I'm lost, I don't know where I am or which way I'm going. Will you please help me to get to the Royal Arms Hotel?"

"I guess you're a her, all right," the driver said, as much to himself as to Jessie. "But I'd sure like to know what kind of a game you're trying to pull on me."

"Please," Jessie said. "This isn't a joke or anything like that. I've got to get to the hotel right away, and I don't have any idea where it is from here."

"Now look, lady," the man went on, "I haven't got time to mess around. I got twenty gallons of milk in this wagon, and folks on my route are going to be wanting it. Why don't you—"

"Listen to me, please," Jessie broke in. "I had some—" She stopped, realizing that at such an hour, dressed

106

as she was, the man would never believe her improbable story. Instead of trying to explain, she said, "I'll pay you well if you'll take me to the Royal Arms."

"How do I know I won't be getting into trouble if I let you get in my wagon?" the milkman asked. "For all I know—"

Jessie had realized the moment she spoke of paying the man that she had no idea whether the clothing she was wearing had any money in any of its pockets. Quickly she plunged her hands into the coat pockets, and found a bulging wallet in the inner breast pocket. Taking the wallet out, she looked at its main compartment and found a thick sheaf of currency.

She took out several of the banknotes and saw that all of them were Canadian and all were of hundred-dollar denomination. She peeled two of the bills off the stack, held them up, and told the milkman, "You can have both of these if you'll just take me to the Royal Arms."

For a moment he stared at the money, then he said, "Well, I don't guess it's none of my business what you been up to. And it won't hurt nobody if I'm a little bit late on my route. Come on, lady. Get in. For that much money, I'll take you anyplace you want to go."

During the ride to the hotel—a very long ride, Jessie discovered—the driver said nothing, though he kept glancing sideways at her. Occasionally he'd sniff, and Jessie again became aware that the scent of the bed on which she'd lain unconscious for so long was still clinging to her. She paid little attention to the man. Her mind was busy sorting out the events of the past twenty-four hours and making plans for the immediate future.

At last the milkwagon reached the hotel, and Jessie paid the driver and went in. The night clerk was half asleep, leaning on the desk with his chin cradled in his hands. Jessie walked fast as she passed him and he paid no attention to her in the few moments before she was out of his sight.

Hurrying up the stairs, Jessie knocked at the door of her suite. Ki opened the door almost instantly. He was still fully dressed in spite of the hour, and she knew he'd stayed awake, waiting for her to return.

"Jessie!" he gasped. "I've been wondering and worrying about you! What happened to you? Where have you been, and why are you wearing a man's suit?"

"It's a long story, Ki, and I'll tell you all of it later. This suit I've got on belonged to Count von Aschenhausen. He was a cartel operative—"

"Was?" Ki broke in.

"I had to kill him. But you'll have to wait to hear the rest. I'm all right, and I've learned a few things that we only suspected before. But we need to move fast now, and there's no time for talking."

After the many hazards he and Jessie had been through together, Ki knew enough not to question her further. He nodded and said, "I can guess part of what's happened, and the rest can wait. What do you plan to do?"

"Leave for the Ojibway country as soon as I can bathe and put on my traveling clothes. How much more do we have to do before we can get started?"

"Very little. Standing Bear and his nephew will be bringing the horses and our trail gear here to the hotel in an hour or less. They'll be ready to travel, of course. Will that be soon enough?"

"An hour's just about as much time as I'll need. We'll have to leave our bags here until we get back, so you can pack them while I'm getting ready. The sooner we can leave, the better. You'll understand why when I've had time to tell you what's been happening."

"I can wait until we're on the trail, Jessie. We'll have

time to talk then. Go on, get ready. I'll take care of what needs to be done now."

"So you see," Jessie said, "we weren't just seeing ghosts under the bed when we talked about the possibility of the cartel's having a hand in this land-grabbing scheme."

Ki nodded soberly. To talk privately, they'd walked a few yards away from the campfire where Standing Bear and his nephew, Mizuan, were cooking supper. They'd left Winnipeg soon after daylight that morning, and had stopped at dusk beside a little singing creek that ran into the Assiniboine River, only a few miles south.

Ki had listened without interrupting while Jessie told him of her encounter with Count von Aschenhausen, then he had said, "I've guessed part of what happened." He took a small fold of paper from his pocket and gave it to Jessie. "I found this when I went through the pockets of the suit you had on when you came back to the hotel this morning."

Jessie unfolded the paper. It was a strip torn from the bottom of a sheet of thick, expensive bond and had only a half-dozen words written on it. Jessie held it up to catch the light from the campfire and looked at it. She did not recognize the handwriting, but the brief message told her that whoever had written the note must be high in the cartel's chain of command. The words were: *Question her. Then kill her.*

"It's from whoever was giving orders to the count," Ki said. "And it might help us run him to earth. Until they find Aschenhausen's body, they might be thrown into enough confusion to give us a good start this time."

"I hope so, Ki. That's why I wanted to start at once. All we have to do now is to find their key men who are doing the dirty work against the Ojibway."

"There can't be that many strangers where we're heading," Jessie said. "Standing Bear and the other Indians should be able to tell us who they are."

"We might be able to spot them ourselves," Ki said thoughtfully. "I think that by now we're able to smell out the cartel's habits. All their schemes seem to follow a pattern."

"Yes. But it's a pattern very few people would believe, Ki. I don't think even Alex would have believed it, if the cartel hadn't tried to get him to join them first."

"But why here in Canada, Jessie, if their target is the United States?"

Instead of replying directly, Jessie gestured with her hand in a wave that took in the country south of them. "That's the reason, Ki. Look at it."

"It looks about like the Texas prairie to me, Jesssie. Flat and level, as far as you can see. The only difference is that if we were in South Texas it wouldn't be green, as this is."

Jessie nodded. "Exactly. Level and green. Ideal for the world's most needed crop. Wheat. And if the cartel can get control of enough wheatland, they'll be able to dictate wheat prices everywhere in the world."

"But why here? Why not farther south, in Minnesota and the Dakota Territory, where there's already a lot of wheat being grown?"

"If they tried to start south of the Canadian border, they'd run into United States homestead laws," Jessie pointed out. "But if they get started up here in Canada, where the laws don't limit them, they can find ways to expand into the States without anybody realizing what's happening."

"That's the same pattern we saw when they were trying to get control of those big ranches in Mexico," Ki observed.

"It goes back to what you said a minute ago," Jessie pointed out. "That's why we can smell them out so often now."

Before Ki could reply, Standing Bear called from the fire. "We have supper ready, if you're hungry."

Standing Bear and Mizuan had dragged logs up on both sides of the fire, and the four sat down and began eating steak and rice with some kind of herb or seasoning that Jessie did not recognize. Whatever it was, it gave the rice a flavor that was much more palatable than its usually flat and uninteresting taste.

"This is the best rice I've ever eaten, Mizuan," Jessie said. "How did you get it so tasty?"

"I put dry bearberries and meat juice in the kettle," the young Ojibway replied. "It makes a good taste with the rice."

"It certainly does," Ki agreed. "My mother's people are rice-eaters too, Mizuan, and this is as good as any I've ever eaten."

"When we get to our village and eat what the old women cook, you will find it even better," Mizuan promised. "There they can cook it with ducks and fish. They give it a finer taste than town meat does."

"Just the same, this is delicious," Jessie said. "I hope you know a lot more dishes as good that you'll cook for us on the way." She put her plate on the log beside her and stood up. "I think I'll go to bed now. I've had a long, busy day, and we've got a lot of ground to cover before we get to your village."

Their journey for the next three days took them from cleared, rolling country into woodland. Late on the third day, after crossing a dozen or more small creeks that flowed into the Assiniboine, Standing Bear led them north, along one of the creeks. Here they entered a more densely wooded country, mile after mile of small, widely spaced trees that thrust up from the dense growth of brush from which rose the thick

111

stumps of bigger, older trees that had fallen years earlier to the logger's ax.

If there were trails through the brush, Jessie could not see them, but Standing Bear kept his horse moving at a steady gait through the dense underbrush until he halted at a spring that gushed from a granite formation near the creek they'd been following.

"We have only a short day's travel tomorrow before we reach our village," he announced. Turning to Jessie, he added, "Then you will learn why we have asked for your help."

Jessie was surprised at the small size of the Ojibway village. It consisted of only a score of two- and three-room dwellings in a clearing that extended southward from the shore of Lake Francis. The lake itself was small in comparison to the huge expanse of Lake Manitoba, which could be seen stretching north beyond the broad spit of land on which the village stood.

To Jessie the village looked very much like the hundreds of tiny settlements she'd seen in her extensive travels through the Western United States. The houses were widely scattered over a semicircular area, and formed a crescent with its tips a bit less than a mile apart. Each house had its own neat garden plot, a well, and a barn that was bigger than the house. The common building, which Jessie soon learned was used by the Ojibway as a town hall and school as well as a place for tribal ceremonies and feasts, stood roughly in the center of the crescent, and radiating from the village, the tribal farmlands stretched as far as Jessie could see.

After a confused hour or so following the party's arrival, when they'd met each of the adults living in the settlement, Jessie was taken by Standing Bear to the community building to meet the other two elders who were responsible for conducting tribal business. Ki stayed with Mizuan, who was delighted to be able to win reflected glory by introducing him to other village residents.

From her conversations with Standing Bear on the way from Texas, Jessie had learned the names of his fellow councillors, but the mental images the names had conjured in her mind had no relationship to the two men themselves.

Migizi, the eldest, was much older than either Standing Bear or the third councillor, Amik. Jessie tried to guess Migizi's age, but found it impossible. In spite of the deep seams that gave his face the appearance of a relief map depicting a dry riverbed, the old man was spry and alert.

Amik, Jessie guessed, was younger than Migizi and older than Standing Bear. He was a stocky man, broad of chest and waist. Both Migizi and Standing Bear had the thin, slightly hooked nose with flaring nostrils that characterized the faces of most of the Ojibway. Amik's face was wide and appeared chubby, his nose fleshier and flatter than those seen on most of the village's inhabitants.

"We thank you for coming to us, Jessie Starbuck," Migizi began formally after they'd settled into chairs. "You honor us and yourself as well, for you are fulfilling a promise that our great benefactor, Alex Starbuck, made before you were born."

"Give the credit to Standing Bear, not to me," Jessie told the old chief. "He was a good messenger for your people, Migizi."

"There are still things that Standing Bear was not able to tell you," Migizi continued, after acknowledging Jessie's remark with a sober nod. "We asked that he wait to tell them to you until you came here, unless it was important to do so in order to persuade you to make the trip."

113

"Jessie Starbuck did not ask many questions," Standing Bear put in when the senior councillor paused. "She is a true daughter of her father."

"These things I speak of, we are ready to tell you now," Migizi went on. "But first we must ask that you pledge secrecy concerning what you will hear."

"I came to help you," Jessie said, "not to reveal your tribal secrets." Then, acting on impulse, she added, "But I hope that what you haven't told me yet will answer a question that's been puzzling me since I first heard of Alex's promise. Does what Standing Bear couldn't talk about have anything to do with the Treasure River?"

All three of the Ojibway looked at her with startled faces. There was a moment of complete silence, then Migizi asked, "Tell me this thing, Jessie Starbuck. How did you learn of Treasure River if Standing Bear did not tell you?"

"I don't really know anything about Treasure River," Jessie confessed. "Just the name. I saw it in the journal that my father kept when he was here with your people."

"You saw nothing but the name?"

Unexpectedly, Standing Bear spoke. "She speaks truth. Jessie Starbuck asked me about the river called Treasure, but as you know, I could tell her nothing."

Migizi nodded. "This is a true thing. It has not been our way to have the secret of Treasure River known to anybody but the elders of the tribal council."

Amik addressed Jessie for the first time since they'd exchanged words of introduction. "I do not know about Treasure River myself, Jessie Starbuck. Neither does Standing Bear. We know of the river, but only its name, and that Migizi must tell one of us its secret before he dies."

"I do not think it is a good thing, what our people have been doing," Migizi said. "It is my plan to tell you and

114

Standing Bear as well, when I explain the river's secret to Jessie Starbuck."

"You have not spoken of this before, Migizi," Standing Bear said slowly. "Are you sure you will not do wrong by changing the way the elders chose so long ago?"

"I have thought much about this thing," the old chief replied. "I have made spirit medicine to guide me. And I have decided that what I will do must be done."

"This is what the spirits your medicine brought told you it is good?" Amik asked.

Migizi nodded. "It is so. Listen to me now, and I will tell you. I know we can trust Jessie Starbuck not to repeat what she will hear, and I know that you, Standing Bear, and you, Amik, will be true to the oath of silence."

With their eyes riveted on the senior councillor, all three waited for him to speak. Migizi took his time, looking from Jessie to Standing Bear to Amik. Then he said, "Treasure River is the—"

Before he could go on, there was an insistent knocking at the door of the council room. Migizi stopped, frowning.

"Who would break our laws and disturb us when we are sitting in council?" he asked of nobody in particular. "Go and see, Amik. Tell whoever it is that we will listen later, after our business is finished."

Amik moved to the door and opened it, the others following him with their eyes. A tall, broad-shouldered man wearing the uniform of the Northwest Mounted Police stood in the doorway. He wore a sergeant's stripes on his red tunic, and his high riding boots, as well as the Sam Browne belt that supported his revolver holster were shining as though they had been polished only minutes earlier.

"Sergeant Lathrop," Amik said, "you know you are always welcome in our village, but we are having a council meeting and cannot be disturbed. If you will wait, we will talk with you later."

"I'm afraid I can't wait for you to finish your business, Chief Beaver," the constable said. "Mine is more important. I came here to make an arrest."

"But surely you can do that without disturbing us," Amik said. "There is no one in here except Standing Bear, Migizi, and an important guest from the United States, Miss Jessie Starbuck."

"That's what I was told," Lathrop nodded, stepping past Amik into the room. He went directly to Jessie and said, "Miss Jessica Starbuck, under the authority vested in me by Her Majesty the Queen, I am placing you under arrest for murder."

Chapter 11

For several seconds there was shocked silence in the room. Migizi was the first to speak. He said, "Sergeant Lathrop, I do not believe what I heard you say."

"I'd advise you to believe me, Chief Bald Eagle," the officer replied. "Even though I'm afraid I can't show you a written warrant, I've orders from Winnipeg to return Miss Starbuck there to stand trial."

During the exchange between Migizi and Lathrop, Jessie's mind had been working at a furious rate. She'd anticipated that when Count von Aschenhausen's body was found, the cartel bosses would see at once that they'd be saved the job of searching for her in the thinly settled Manitoba backcountry by engineering her arrest, but she was surprised that the Mounted Police had found her so soon. She'd counted on the isolation of the Ojibway village to delay both the cartel and the authorities in their search.

Knowing that once she'd been returned to the provincial capital the cartel would be able to send a hired killer into any jail in which she might be confined, Jessie decided that she must stall for time. Almost at once she saw a way she could do so by using the system of justice that was in effect in England itself as well as throughout the British Empire, and which, she'd learned long ago, wherever the British flag flew, law officers were sworn to uphold. Before someone else could break the silence that followed the Mountie's reply, Jessie spoke quickly.

"Just who am I accused of murdering, Sergeant?" she asked.

"A man named Aschenhausen. Count Wilhelm von Aschenhausen, the telegram from Winnipeg said," Lathrop replied.

"And where and when did this murder take place?" Jessie prodded.

"I can't say, Miss Starbuck. The wire from headquarters didn't give all the details."

"And I suppose it didn't give the name of whoever accused me of killing this man?"

Lathrop shook his head. "No. But that information will all be given in the arrest warrant."

"I see. But didn't I hear you tell Migizi that you have no written warrant for my arrest?" she went on relentlessly.

Lathrop's bronzed, clear-cut face showed his reluctance to answer, and his voice echoed his feeling when he replied, "I—I think I did make that statement, ma'am."

"Without a written warrant, I'm afraid I must refuse to go with you, Sergeant Lathrop," Jessie said. "I'm not familiar with Canadian laws, but I assume they're much the same as those in England. And I'm sure you know that under British law, anyone arrested, especially on a charge such as murder, must be shown the written warrant authorizing his or her arrest."

"You seem very well informed about the laws of arrest, Miss Starbuck," the Mountie said.

"I've been advised on them before, by very good attorneys," Jessie said calmly. "I am correct that the law requires you to have a written warrant, am I not?"

"You are indeed. The one thing you didn't mention is

that the warrant must be duly signed by the judge who authorized it," Lathrop replied.

"And you admit that you don't have such a warrant, Sergeant?" she repeated. "I want to be sure that these witnesses hear your answer."

"I'm afraid I don't have one," he agreed.

"Then, with all due respect to your badge and uniform, I don't consider that I'm under arrest," Jessie said, her voice as matter-of-fact as though the fate of some third party were being discussed. She went on, "When you bring me the warrant required by law, Sergeant Lathrop, I'll go with you. Until you show it to me, though, I intend to stay here and go about my business."

"Please don't make my job any harder than it already is, Miss Starbuck," Lathrop said.

"It's you who've put yourself into such an uncomfortable position," she pointed out. "I'm only insisting on my rights under your own laws."

"That doesn't change the fact that a warrant for your arrest on a murder charge has been issued in proper form by a magistrate," he countered.

"And it doesn't change the fact that you don't have the warrant, and can't serve it," Jessie replied.

Lathrop was silent for a moment, then he sighed and said, "I'm afraid you're going to force me to stay here in the village, where I can watch you and make sure you won't try to escape."

"What you do is your own concern, not mine," Jessie told the Mountie coolly. "Now, you interrupted an important meeting, Sergeant Lathrop. Perhaps you'll be good enough to go and let us continue it."

Making no effort to hide his chagrin, the Mountie turned away from the council house door. Jessie closed it and said to the council members, "We can go about our business

119

now. Migizi, you were just starting to tell us about Treasure River."

Migizi said nothing for a few moments, then he shook his head, his face sober. "I cannot do that now, Jessie Starbuck. We are a law-abiding people. Unless you can explain what the man from the Mounted Police told us, I must stay silent about a thing of such importance."

"What she has done or has not done before she came here is not important, Migizi," Standing Bear protested. "That is a matter which concerns only Jessie Starbuck."

"What concerns her at this minute concerns all of us," Migizi insisted. "Amik, do you agree with me?"

"I think I must, Migizi," Amik said. "We do not know what has caused her troubles with the police, but neither do we know what she might be forced to tell them."

Jessie said quickly, "I don't deny that I killed a man in Winnipeg, Migizi. Standing Bear knows about it. So does Ki. But I killed him because he attacked me."

"And this had nothing to do with your coming here?" Migizi insisted, turning to face Jessie.

Looking at the wizened old chief, Jessie wished she could reassure him, but would not lie to him. Swallowing her disappointment, she said, "It does and it doesn't, Migizi. But I think you're right. You should not tell me your secret until the matter's been straightened out."

"How long would this take?" he asked.

"I don't know," Jessie replied. "I might have to go back to Winnipeg for a few days to clear myself."

"Then, when you have done that we will meet again and I will tell you and Hitaze Noka and Amik about the river," Migizi promised. "But none of us must mention it to others." When all three had nodded their agreement, he went on, "Now we will end this meeting. All of us have other work to do."

120

As they left the council room, Jessie saw Sergeant Lathrop a short distance away, sitting on a stump, watching the door. She started toward him, but had taken only a few steps when Ki came rushing up.

"What's this I heard about you being arrested, Jessie?" he asked. "I don't see any—"

Jessie indicated Lathrop with a quick gesture visible only to Ki. He flicked his eyes in the Mountie's direction.

"It's true, then" Ki asked.

"Yes. The cartel's been busy as usual, Ki. They must have called in the police as soon as someone found the count's body. Remember, I had to ask more questions than I'd planned to when we were at the bank, so through Aschenhausen the cartel's known enough from the beginning to guess what we were planning."

"So the Mountie's waiting to arrest you?"

"Not exactly," Jessie answered. "I turned the law to our own use, Ki. I challenged his right to arrest me without serving a written warrant."

"Do you think that's going to hold him off very long?"

"No. I'm sure I'll be arrested soon, but I've managed to keep him from taking me to Winnipeg for a few days. We need a little time to plan our next moves."

"Then I'd better tell Mizuan and Watomi that I can't go with them now," Ki said, glancing over his shoulder.

Jessie looked in the direction of Ki's glance and saw Standing Bear's nephew and a girl a short distance away. She asked, "Where were you going?"

"Oh, we were just going to walk around the village while they showed me the lay of the land. It's not something I need to do right now. As you said, we need to plan."

"Go with them, Ki. It might be a good thing for you to know what the terrain's like around here, and I want to talk to Sergeant Lathrop. We can plan later."

"Whatever suits you best, Jessie," Ki replied. "Shall we talk this evening, after supper?"

"Yes. Maybe we'll both know more after you've spent some time with your friends and I've talked to the sergeant."

When Ki left, Jessie walked toward the Mountie. Lathrop rose as she approached. He was taller and broader than Jessie had realized. During their brief encounter earlier, she'd been too engrossed in planning her moves to give much attention to his appearance. Lathrop was younger than he'd seemed before, in his late twenties or early thirties. He carried himself like a man used to action, and his broad shoulders and sturdy build indicated that he could hold his own in the wilderness.

"I hope you're coming to tell me you've changed your mind about going with me," he said.

"I'm afraid not, Sergeant," she answered. "It's very important to my plans that I stay here. Besides that, going to Winnipeg would just be a waste of both your time and mine. I can prove quite easily that there aren't any grounds for holding me on a charge of murder."

"If that's true, then you've nothing to worry about, Miss Starbuck. You shouldn't resist arrest and delay your chance to give your proof in court."

"Oh, I'm not resisting you," Jessie replied quickly. "But my business here is too important to allow such a groundless charge to interfere with it. I came here to help these Ojibway, and to do that I have to be free to move around."

"Freedom's always very important to somebody who's about to lose it," Lathrop replied. "I can understand that you don't want to go to prison, but as you've proved so cleverly, the law is still the law."

"Setting the law aside for a moment, there's no reason for us to be angry with each other," Jessie said. "I'll admit I'm curious about something. How on earth did you manage

122

to find me here in the backwoods in such a short time?"

"Oh, Canada's not quite the wilderness that you people from the States think it is, Miss Starbuck," he replied.

"I'm not so sure of that," Jessie told him. "It took more than three days for me to get here from Winnipeg. I don't see how you could have gotten orders to arrest me so quickly."

"There's no mystery about that. The Canadian Pacific Railroad is building tracks north from Winnipeg, and the telegraph wire that the railroad's putting up is already in operation as far as my station."

"Just where is your station?"

"To the east, not quite a day's ride. It's at a little settlement called Deer Horn. It doesn't take as long as it once did to get a message from headquarters to my post."

"That still doesn't explain how your headquarters in the capital managed to identify me so quickly," Jessie frowned.

"I must caution you about making any kind of statement to me in connection with your case, Miss Starbuck," Lathrop said quickly. "It can be used as evidence against you when you stand trial."

"I'm not as concerned about standing trial as I am about my enemies who know my whereabouts," Jessie replied.

"Who are these enemies, Miss Starbuck?"

"I think I'll follow your advice and refuse to discuss my case with you, Sergeant. I will say this much, though. It's my guess that they're just using your force to find out where I am by accusing me of murder."

"I find that very hard to believe," Lathrop said. "We aren't amateurs on the force, you know. If any criminal tried to use us to gain his own ends, I'm sure we'd be aware of it."

"I wish I could be so sure," Jessie said. "But time means a great deal right now." She paused, frowning thoughtfully, then went on, "You said there are trains running from your post to Winnipeg now. If I agreed to go with you, how long would the trip take?"

"I don't think I made myself clear," Lathrop said. "It's a good half-day's ride to my post, and from there another half-day to the head of the tracks. Even if I got permission to bring you in myself, instead of waiting for a bailiff to come from Winnipeg to fetch you, it might be a week before we got there."

And that week would give one of the cartel's murder squads more than enough time to get here, Jessie told herself. She said to Lathrop, "Let me be sure I understand you, Sergeant. In order to send word to Winnipeg, won't you have to go back to your post so that you can wire your headquarters?"

"I can't very well send a wire from here, can I?"

"You'll be gone for two days, then," Jessie pointed out. "Suppose I decide to leave before you get back?"

"Don't play me for a fool, Miss Starbuck," Lathrop warned her, his voice stern. "I have no intention of leaving here without taking you into custody."

"On what charge?" she countered.

"Murder, of course."

"But you just said—"

Lathrop broke in. "Miss Starbuck," he said patiently. "I advise you to stop thinking of the Northwest Mounted Police as a band of backwoods yokels. I didn't say I intended to arrest you. I'll have one of the Ojibway men take a written message to Deer Horn. My clerk will telegraph it to Winnipeg, and headquarters will send the arrest warrant up by the first train."

"That means you're going to be here several days?"

"Of course. And I'll be watching you very closely to see that you don't disappear while I'm waiting."

"I have no intention of disappearing, Sergeant Lathrop.

In fact, I would like to ask you to send a message for me at the same time yours goes to Winnipeg."

Lathrop was thoughtfully silent for a moment, then he said, "I'm not sure my headquarters would approve of my using our telegraph to send a message for a prisoner."

Her voice suddenly icy, Jessie said, "You've forgotten that I haven't been arrested yet, Sergeant. Or do you plan to arrest me now?"

Lathrop's face reddened. He said, "My apologies, Miss Starbuck. I'm afraid I spoke without thinking."

"An understandable mistake, I suppose," Jessie observed, her voice still chilly. When Lathrop did not answer, Jessie went on, "Since I'm still a free woman and not your prisoner, I think I must insist that you show me the courtesy of sending the messages I've requested."

"I'll be very glad to accommodate you, Miss Starbuck," the Mountie said, his voice showing nothing except reluctance. "But I'll have to ask you to whom they'll be addressed before I can say for sure."

"You can see who they're addressed to when I give them to you, of course," Jessie pointed out. "But I don't mind telling you in advance. One will be to Winnipeg; it will be addressed to Lord Brereton at the Royal Bank of Manitoba. The other must be sent to Quebec. It will go to the Earl of Kimberly. I believe you'll recognize the name. The earl is still the Governor-General of Canada, is he not?"

★

Chapter 12

When Sergeant Lathrop heard the names of two of the most powerful men in Canada, he stared at Jessie, his mouth open in surprise. At last he said, "I'm tempted to call your bluff and send those wires, Miss Starbuck. I suppose you're acquainted with both Lord Brereton and the Governor-General?"

"Of course." Jessie shrugged. "If I didn't know them, I certainly wouldn't be foolish enough to send them telegrams."

"You're suggesting that you know them well enough to ask them to intervene in this case?"

"I've met Lord Brereton only recently," Jessie replied. "I want to assure him that I don't blame him for introducing me to Count von Aschenhausen. Or perhaps you didn't know that the count was one of Lord Brereton's assistants?"

"I have no idea what the count did, or where he worked, or even that he worked at all," Lathrop admitted.

"As for the Earl of Kimberly," Jessie went on, "he was a business associate of my father's. He's been a guest at my ranch in Texas, and before my father's death we visited him at one of his estates in Scotland. I'm sure he'll be interested in knowing that I've been arrested in Canada before a complete investigation has been made of the crime I'm accused of committing."

"Now just a minute, Miss Starbuck!" Lathrop protested. "The Mounted Police don't issue arrest warrants unless there's enough evidence to justify them!"

"If a warrant's been issued, you haven't seen it," Jessie reminded him. "And I haven't, either. Until I've seen the evidence supporting the warrant, I'm not going to be foolish enough to act on guesswork."

"Are you calling me a fool?" Lathrop asked angrily.

"Not at all," Jessie said levelly. "Overeager, perhaps, but certainly not a fool. This arrest is simply an effort to keep me from doing what I came here to do."

"I'm still not clear exactly why you did come here," the Mountie said.

"To help the Ojibways keep their tribal lands from being gobbled up by a group of land-grabbers."

"From what you said a minute ago, I got the impression that you live on a ranch in Texas. Isn't this a long way to travel, just to help some Indians you've never seen before?"

"I inherited an obligation from my father to help the Ojibways, Sergeant Lathrop. He'd have wanted me to come here."

Lathrop nodded and murmured, "I see."

To Jessie it was obvious that he didn't, but she decided at once that a full explanation would take a great deal of time and require her to explain the power-grabbing efforts of the cartel. She wasn't sure that even then the Mountie would believe her.

She said, "As long as I have to fight a trumped-up murder charge, I can't get on with my job. I need to be free to move when the time comes."

Lathrop frowned. "You mentioned land-grabbers. I

127

haven't seen any evidence that they're operating here in Manitoba."

"You'll see the evidence later, when they get control of the land farther south, and can stop the flow of streams that the people here depend on to provide water for their crops."

"I'm beginning to think you're serious about all this, Miss Starbuck," the sergeant said. "If what you say is true, then you're better informed than I am about what's happening."

"It's true enough, and I hope I'm convincing you that it is," Jessie told him. "Now I have a suggestion that might save us a great deal of time, if you're willing to listen to it."

"Go ahead. You'll find I'm a reasonable man."

"Suppose I go with you to your post. You send a telegram to your headquarters and tell them you must have the arrest warrant. I'll wire the Governor-General and Lord Brereton."

Lathrop waited, but Jessie had stopped talking and was watching him expectantly. He said, "You haven't told me what you're going to say in your wires, Miss Starbuck."

"I'll tell them that what I'm doing here is too important to be interrupted, and ask the Governor-General to have delivery of the warrant suspended for a few days. Lord Brereton heads the bank from which I'd draw funds if I ran short. I want him to have extra money ready for me if I need it."

"It sounds to me as though you're suggesting a truce," the sergeant muttered.

Jessie shrugged. "If you want to call it that. I'm not going to run away. I doubt that I'd get far if I tried, because I'm sure you know the country better than Ki and I do."

For a moment Lathrop stood thinking, then he nodded. "I'll accept your suggestion," he said. "I'd have to take you to my post anyhow, to put you on the train to Winnipeg.

128

As for your wires—well, I'll suspend judgment on them until I see what results we get from your message to the Governor-General."

"I think you're being very fair, Sergeant," Jessie said. "I'm ready to leave whenever you are."

After a quick glance at the sky, Lathrop said, "There's about two hours of daylight left. If you don't mind traveling the last part of the way at night, we can leave now. The train from Winnipeg usually gets to rail-end early in the morning, and it's quite a ride from the construction camp to my station."

"I can't see any reason to wait," Jessie told him. "I'm not a bit afraid of the dark."

"There's only one thing more," Lathrop said quickly. "I'll have to ask you to surrender that Colt you have in your holster. I'm sure you haven't any intention of using it, but I'm risking my badge in following your plan, and I don't want to get out on a limb any further than I can help."

"Of course," Jessie agreed. She unbuckled her gunbelt and handed it to the Mountie, then she went on, "Now. When do we start, Sergeant?"

"As soon as you're ready."

"Give me a minute to talk with Ki," Jessie replied. "Then we can be on our way."

Dawn had given way to full daylight, and the sun was fully above the eastern horizon when Jessie came into the office of the Deer Horn Mounted Police station the next morning. The office was the largest room in the station; it extended across one side of the building and was perhaps ten feet wide. Doors to the station's three small bedrooms and kitchen took up most of the back wall. The room's two small rectangular windows were set high in the outer wall, on either side of the door.

Lathrop was sitting at a scarred and much-used desk in one corner. He was coatless, though the three stripes of his rank were sewn on the sleeve of his shirt. His scarlet coat hung over the back of his chair, and his Sam Browne belt with its holstered .41 Webley revolver hung over the coat. He did not stand when Jessie entered, but looked up and said, "Good morning, Miss Starbuck. I hope you slept well."

"Very well indeed, Sergeant. And very late too, which is unusual for me. At home, on the ranch, I'm used to getting up before sunrise."

"But I doubt that you've ridden half the night before," he said. "Yesterday was a long day, Miss Starbuck."

Jessie nodded, then said, "Sergeant Lathrop, since we'll be together here for the next day or so, I'd really prefer to be less formal. Do you think you could overlook any professional scruples you might have about being familiar with a prisoner—or someone who might be your prisoner—and call me Jessie?"

"I'm not as straitlaced as you seem to think," Lathrop replied. "I'll be glad to. And I'm called by my rank or last name so much that I almost forget my first name. It's Ben."

"Good. Now where is your town? Deer Horn, isn't it? I looked out my window, but I didn't see it."

"Small wonder, Jessie. Deer Horn's two miles away."

"What am I going to do for breakfast, then? After biscuits and jerky on the trail last night, I've been famished since I first woke up."

"My fault, that was," Lathrop grimaced. "I left for the Ojibway village yesterday in such a hurry that I didn't put fresh provisions in my saddlebags. But we have a kitchen. I'd offer my services, but my clerk does the cooking, and I started him to town for supplies as soon as he was out of bed."

"Not before you sent our telegrams, I hope."

"Oh, I did that last night before I turned in."

"You've very efficient, Ben."

"You don't stay on the force long if you aren't," Lathrop told her. He went on, "Now then. Breakfast. There's a pot of coffee on the stove, bread and bacon in the larder, and some eggs. Can you cook, or shall I fix them for you?"

"I'm a very good cook. If you'll show me which door leads to the kitchen, I'll be glad to look after myself."

Jessie did not hurry over breakfast. She sat in the kitchen and sipped a second cup of coffee after she'd finished eating, and washed the plate and cup she'd used before going back into the station office. Lathrop was still sitting at his desk, going through a large stack of mail.

"This is what I wasn't here to take care of yesterday," he said. "And I know today's train will bring this much more."

"I have the same thing at the ranch. We have a long ride to the railroad, too."

"In another three or four months we'll have rails all the way to the post, and it'll be a real treat to sit in a passenger car and ride all the way to Winnipeg. But it's better now than when I was first stationed here, four years ago. Then I had to go all the way on horseback."

"Canada's growing fast, I know," Jessie said. "But—" She stopped and cocked her head to listen, then said, "I suppose that horse I hear is your clerk coming back."

Lathrop listened too, then shook his head. "No. Those are two horses, not one. And they're coming from the south."

"From the railroad?"

"More than likely," Lathrop said as he rose from his chair and went to one of the small windows. He went on, "The train from Winnipeg must've gotten to railhead. Those riders are two of our constables." He watched them for a moment and grunted. "Hmph. Either they're new, from the training academy in Quebec, or transfers from some station in another province. I've never seen either of them before."

Striding to the door, Lathrop swung it open. Jessie came to look over his shoulder at the new arrivals. They wore the Northwest Mounted Police uniform, broad-brimmed hats with a modified Montana crease, scarlet coats, whipcord riding pants, and high boots, both the boots and their Sam Browne belts polished to a slick shine.

As the newcomers reined in at the hitch rail, Lathrop said, "Come in, men. I guess you know who I am, but I don't recall having met either of you."

"We're new at the Winnipeg headquarters, Sergeant," one of them said as they swung out of the saddle and came to the door. "I'm Carson, he's Rogers. You'd be Ben Lathrop, of course."

"You didn't have to guess to know that," Lathrop told them as he stepped back to let them enter, then moved to his desk and sat down. "What brings you up here? Headquarters didn't wire me that I'd be having visitors."

"They should have," Carson said. "But I suppose one of the clerks is late in getting the message off."

"That doesn't happen often," Lathrop said. "But I suppose it'll get here during the course of the day."

"Things are a bit upset at headquarters," Rogers put in. "I'm sure you'll get the wire later. We've come to take custody of a prisoner you're holding, a woman named Starbuck, charged with murder. Our orders are to bring her back to Winnipeg."

"I suppose she's in your holdover cell," Rogers asked, his eyes fixed on Jessie.

"You can save asking any more questions," she broke in. "I'm Jessie Starbuck."

Rogers turned back to Lathrop. "I'm surprised, Sergeant. Here you are holding a murderess, and you don't take even

132

the most elementary precautions! But don't worry, Carson and I aren't informers."

A faint frown had begun to form on the sergeant's face when Rogers announced why he and Carson were there. The frown grew deeper as Lathrop listened, then suddenly it vanished and he said, "Miss Starbuck isn't locked up because there's been a mixup over the arrest warrant. In fact, I sent a telegraph message to Colonel Ferol last night, explaining it and asking him to straighten it out."

"Mixup?" Carson frowned. "What mixup?"

"This is the first we've heard about anything of that sort," Rogers volunteered.

"That's odd," Lathrop told him, looking from one to the other of the men. "What time did you men leave Winnipeg?"

"Why, at the usual time the work train goes every morning," Carson replied. "About three o'clock."

"My message went out before eleven o'clock last night," Lathrop said. "Tabbed 'urgent' and marked for Colonel Ferol's attention. It should've been delivered to him at once, at home, if he'd left the office, just as all urgent messages are."

Jessie was watching Lathrop and the two new arrivals with a frown growing on her face. She said, "Perhaps you'd better send another message to the colonel. I'm not changing my mind just because these two men have come to take me back to Winnipeg. I still insist—"

"Shut up, Miss Starbuck!" Lathrop snapped. "Don't forget your position! You're a prisoner now, not a rich woman who can make everybody jump when you snap your fingers! This is something we'll straighten out among ourselves!"

For a moment Jessie stood in silent astonishment at the sudden change in Lathrop's attitude. She started to speak, then caught the significance of the frown that puckered the corners of his eyes.

133

Lathrop turned back to the new arrivals. He asked, "You said you left Winnipeg at three this morning?"

"About that," Carson answered.

Lathrop nodded, his face expressionless. "I'm sure the colonel must've gotten my message," he said. "He probably felt it wasn't important enough to answer." Walking the few steps to his desk, he sat down and looked at Jessie with a scowl. He pointed his forefinger at her and cocked his thumb back like a revolver hammer and wagged his hand at her as he went on, "I'll be glad to get rid of you! You've done nothing but annoy me since I arrested you!" Turning to Rogers, he said, "Go on. Get her out of my sight!"

"Fine," Rogers said. "We've arranged for the train to wait until we get back before it starts its return to Winnipeg, so we won't waste any more time."

Carson produced a pair of handcuffs. "Even if you don't think she's dangerous enough for cuffs, I'm not going to take any chances." He turned to Jessie and went on, "Hold out your hands. And if you're smart, you won't give us any trouble."

Jessie looked at Lathrop. He met her eyes squarely, then let one eyelid droop a tiny fraction of an inch. Then he said, "Oh, by the way, you'll want to take her gun with you. It might be needed as evidence."

Opening his desk drawer, he took out Jessie's Colt. He slid it out of the holster, saying as he did so, "You know, I wouldn't mind having this gun myself. It's a very fancy job."

Rogers stepped forward with his hand extended to take the Colt from Lathrop. Instead of handing it to him, the sergeant tossed it to Jessie as he said, "They're imposters, Jessie! Don't let either one get close to you!"

When he tossed the Colt, both Rogers and Carson were totally surprised. They stood with open mouths, gazing at the revolver as it sailed through the air. Not until Lathrop called to Jessie did they grasp what was happening. By then it was too late.

Without waiting to see whether Jessie had succeeded in catching the weapon, Lathrop grabbed for the holster containing his Webley. In spite of the buckled flap over the gun's butt, he had the Webley out of its holster before Carson and Rogers—or whoever they really were—could reach for their own weapons. By that time Jessie's hand had closed firmly on the familiar grips of her Colt.

Carson had pulled away the butt-flap of his holster and was drawing his weapon when Jessie fired. The slug from her revolver smashed through his skull into his brain.

Before Rogers could get his pistol out of its holster, Lathrop's shot followed Jessie's. The fake Mountie's body jerked back as the heavy bullet from the Webley tore into his chest. He crumpled to the floor only seconds after Carson had collapsed in a motionless heap.

It was Lathrop who broke the silence that fell over the office after the blasts echoed into silence. He told Jessie, "I couldn't give you any kind of warning when I realized those two were imposters. I just had to trust that you'd understand in time to get a shot off."

"I wondered about them for a few minutes after they first came in," she replied. "Then you seemed to accept them, and their uniforms looked just like yours—"

"Small wonder they did," Lathrop broke in. "They're our official uniforms, all right. I can't be fooled about that. But I'm sure we'll find out they were stolen."

"But they sounded like they knew what was going on, until you mentioned the arrest warrant," she said. "I was puzzled until I caught your signal. It took me a minute to realize you were trying to tell me you'd throw my Colt to me."

"It took me longer than a minute to figure out how to handle things. As soon as I realized they were fakes, I tried to think of a way to reach my desk without making them suspicious."

"You mean they didn't fool you at all, Ben?"

"No. You see, Jessie, we Mounties started out as a very small force, just as your Texas Rangers did. And we developed the same tradition the Rangers have, that no matter how big a job is, one Mountie should be able to handle it without having to call for help. There isn't an officer on our force who'd send two men to return a prisoner. It simply isn't done."

"I see," Jessie replied abstractedly.

While she'd been listening to Lathrop, her mind had been working busily. That the cartel would risk trying to take her from the custody of the Mounted Police could mean only one thing: its bosses had planned a new and major move in Canada, some kind of action that could be endangered if she was free to move around. Coming as it did on the heels of Aschenhausen's effort to murder her, there could be no other explanation for the elaborate and even riskier attempt that had just failed.

Lathrop noted her changed manner and asked, "Is something wrong, Jessie?"

"I was thinking," she said quickly. Then she went on, "I wonder if there's anything in those fake Mounties' pockets that might help us find out who sent them?"

"We'll soon find out," Lathrop told her.

He bent over the bodies, first Carson, then Rogers, and quickly rifled their pockets. There was nothing in the pockets of Carson's tunic or trousers except a few coins and a

136

wad of currency, but from the breast pocket of Rogers's coat, he produced a folded paper.

As he began opening its creases, Jessie was struck by the similarity it had to the slip that Ki had found in Aschenhausen's coat. It was the same thick, creamy bond paper. Lathrop took a quick look at it and handed it to Jessie. She recognized the same bold, flowing script that she'd seen in the other note.

Starbuck woman's recapture essential to our attack plan, she read. *Success will be rewarded, failure punished.* There was no signature on the note.

★

Chapter 13

"Do you have any idea who wrote this?" Lathrop asked Jessie. "Or who it was sent to?"

Jessie had been asked such questions before, by people who knew nothing of the cartel and its sinister plans. She'd found that her efforts to explain brought only stares of disbelief and a flood of additional questions. To anyone reared in the United States, Canada, or Mexico, the idea that there was a European cartel trying to take over the key resources of the entire North American continent was totally inconceivable.

"I wish I did," she said. "But it's obviously instructions to the land-grabbers."

"But what kind of attack?" the Mountie persisted. "Against whom, besides you?"

"I'm sure the Ojibway village is their next target," Jessie replied. "The village councillors said the land-grabbers have been moving in from the west, so they'd be next in line."

"Jessie, I've got a feeling that you know more about these land-grabbers than you've told me," Lathrop said.

"I suspect a number of things, Ben," she replied. "But I don't really know anything, certainly can't prove anything."

"How did you happen to get involved in this? Texas is a long way from Canada."

"My father was interested in lumbering a long time ago. He bought timberland in this part of Canada, and when he'd harvested the trees he gave the land to the Ojibways for farming."

"So they asked you for help in keeping their lands?"

"Yes. I felt responsible. After all, it was Alex who was instrumental in settling the Ojibways where they are."

"Well, at least I know now why you came here. I can't understand how you've learned so much about this bunch you call land-grabbers, though."

"Perhaps you just don't think of them by that name. In gold-mining country they'd be called claim jumpers," Jessie said.

"That's a term I do understand," Lathrop agreed. "And it might explain something I've noticed lately in my district."

"What's that?" Jessie asked.

"There've been more farms sold here than ever before."

Jessie nodded. "Some of the sales may have been forced."

"If they have been, we haven't had any complaints."

"Do you think they'd come and tell you, Ben? You know how Indians value what they call 'face.' They'd lose a lot of face if they came to the Mounted Police with a complaint like that."

"But from the way this note reads, it's not just a case of harassing a few Indians," Lathrop protested. "Whoever wrote it used the word 'attack.'"

"That might mean they're changing tactics," Jessie said thoughtfully. "They've learned that trying to bully individual farmers is too slow, and they're going to see if they can get a whole village to give up."

"Damn it, Jessie, that kind of thing ended fifty years

ago! Canada's not that kind of country any longer!"

"Just the same, this note worries me," Jessie said. "I have a feeling that when Ki and I got here, we started the land-grabbers thinking about using violence on a large scale."

"You've tangled with them before, I take it," Lathrop said. "I'd like to know where and when."

Jessie evaded his effort to get specific details. She said only, "I've run into them a few times. Some of the people who hated my father have passed their dislike on to me."

"Is that why the Ojibway came to you and asked for help?"

"Partly, yes. You know how news spreads. It travels very fast, even in unsettled country like this. Don't forget, the Indians were sending smoke signals and drum messages long before we came along with mail service and the telegraph."

"We'd better get back to the village, then," Lathrop said. "Maybe I was wrong to leave it."

"There's still the arrest warrant to think about," Jessie reminded him.

"That can wait, unless you have some objections. And now that you've got your pistol back, I think you'd better keep it. What's just happened convinces me that somebody really is trying to get you out of the way."

"And these two?" Jessie indicated the bodies of the cartel agents.

"My clerk ought to be back from Deer Horn by the time we get ready to leave. He can do what's necessary."

"Then let's get ready to go while we're waiting for him," Jessie said. "There's no use in wasting any time."

If there was any danger threatening the Ojibway village, Jessie and Lathrop saw no signs as they drew close to it on their ride back. It was midafternoon when they came within

140

sight of the settlement, and in the fields surrounding the little half-moon of houses the men and women were working peacefully.

When they reached the zigzag trail that skirted the plots of cultivated ground, Lathrop said, "I've been thinking, Jessie. It seems to me that because the Ojibways have such a high opinion of your father, you'd have more influence with them than I would in persuading them to stand off an attack."

Jessie understood the Mountie's reasoning at once. The village people were more likely to accept her suggestions, since she was Alex Starbuck's daughter, than those given by a policeman who was forced at times to enforce laws that they found unpopular.

"I'll do what I can, of course. But what will your head-quarters think about your trusting a job like that to me? I'm almost a fugitive from a murder charge."

"I'll worry about that later. I'm sure Colonel Ferol will see my reasoning when I explain. Besides, it's getting late in the day, and I've got to scout around and see if I can turn up any signs that trouble's nearby."

"I'll go on to the village, then, and do what I can to start getting a defense organized."

Jessie went on alone, and as she drew closer to the village, Ki saw her and waved. He was waiting to greet her when she dismounted in front of the council house.

"What happened?" he asked Jessie. "I didn't look for you to get back this soon. I thought you were about to be arrested and taken to Winnipeg."

Knowing that Ki could fill in the gaps from his own knowledge of the cartel's operations, Jessie gave him an abbreviated account of what had happened since she'd gone with Lathrop to the Mountie's station.

"So that's why we came back," she concluded, after

winding up her account with the quick gunfight between her and Lathrop and the cartel's operatives. Then she asked, "Has anything unusual been happening here?"

"No. Mizuan and some of his friends have been taking me around the area. I thought it might be a good idea to learn the lay of the land."

"If what I suspect is true, whatever you've learned might come in very handy," she agreed. "I think we'd better find Migizi and Amik and Standing Bear, and have a talk with them as soon as possible."

"You're looking for trouble right away?" Ki asked.

"It seems to me that I've been a magnet for trouble since we got to Canada," Jessie replied. "I don't think there's been any change in the last twenty-four hours."

"You'd probably like to rest after your ride," Ki told her. "I'll go find Shining Water and Mizuan. He'll know where Standing Bear is, and Watomi can help me find her father."

"Watomi?"

"Amik's daughter. Her English name is Shining Water."

Jessie nodded. "I see. Go ahead, then. I'll wait here by the council house."

For the next half hour Jessie waited impatiently, seeing the sun drop still lower in the west. Then Amik arrived, followed soon afterward by Standing Bear and Migizi. The senior chief asked Jessie, "You have no more troubles with the police now, Jessie Starbuck?"

"Not for the moment. But the same enemies that have been trying to harm me may be preparing trouble for your village."

"How is this possible? Why should they trouble us? We live in peace with everyone, we trouble nobody."

"Some men have more than their share of greed, Migizi. The men who want more land here are after your farms."

"But we were given the land by your father!" the old

chief protested. "He promised that it would be ours as long as the sky is blue and the sun shines each morning from the east!"

"There are times when all of us have to fight to keep what has been given us," Jessie reminded him.

"You say we may have to fight, but you have not said when," Standing Bear put in.

"I don't know when, Standing Bear," Jessie replied. "But soon, maybe as soon as tomorrow."

"We are not fighters," Amik said, shaking his head sadly. "When the great sickness so many years ago killed all but a handful of our young warriors, we were driven from our old lands to where we are now because we could not fight as fiercely as the Mohawk and Seneca and others of the Algonkin. Today we have forgotten how to fight at all."

"Even if we had much time to train our young men, they would still not have the skill or weapons," Migizi said.

"How many guns do you have?" Ki asked.

"We have a few flintlocks that were used by our forefathers, and perhaps three or four new rifles," Migizi replied.

Jessie had been listening with increasing dismay. She said, "Surely those who have guns know how to use them."

Again Migizi shook his head. "Only the old men like us, who learned when we were young. We have learned to trade for our food instead of killing it. Most of the guns have not been fired for many years. And I do not know how many of those who have guns will also have powder and bullets for them."

Jessie turned to Standing Bear. She said, "I know you have a good rifle and ammunition for it. Will you go through the village and see how many of the men have weapons they can use?"

"I will do my best," Standing Bear replied. "But Migizi

has told you the truth. We do not have enough weapons to stand off the land-grabbers, if they attack us."

"Sergeant Lathrop came back with me," Jessie told the councilmen. "He has a rifle and a pistol, and I have a pistol. We'll fight beside you if they do attack you."

Turning to Ki, Standing Bear asked, "Will you fight too?"

"Of course," Ki replied quickly. "But I have my own way of fighting. I do not use a gun."

Migizi's face had drawn into a thoughtful frown. He said, "Ki, our young people must help too. Will you teach them as much as you can, and lead them if we are forced to fight?"

"There's not much time, but I'll do what I can," Ki told him. "And if we're going to fight, we'd better stop talking about what we plan to do, and begin getting ready to do it."

The council broke up at once, Standing Bear to scour the settlement for usable guns, while Migizi and Amik began assembling the young men and older boys in the council house for Ki to teach. Jessie and Ki stopped outside the door to talk privately.

"Can you really teach these Ojibway boys enough for them to help us?" she asked.

"I can't make masters of them in a few hours, you know that, Jessie," Ki replied. "But I can give them a will to fight and show them a few attacks."

"I can't even guess what Ben's going to find," Jessie said with a thoughtful frown. "I'd better go look for him right now. There's not more than two or three hours of daylight left. You stay here and start training the young men."

Jessie was approaching the edge of the Ojibways' cultivated land when she saw Lathrop. He was emerging from a brush thicket near the edge of the lake, and she stood up in her stirrups and waved to catch his attention. He returned her wave and turned his horse in her direction. They met beside a field of sprouting wheat, its tender young shoots rippling in the light breeze off the lake.

"I'd like to know where your hunches come from, Jessie," he greeted her as they reined in. "I didn't see anybody, but I came across fresh tracks of two wagons that circled around the village far enough away so they wouldn't be seen."

"And you followed the tracks?"

"No. But I'm sure I know where they're heading. There's a dry riverbed just a few miles to the southwest. I'm sure that's where they'll camp. I figured the best thing I could do was get back here and tell the Ojibways to be ready."

"Do you think they'll attack tomorrow?"

"More than likely. They wouldn't wait another day, there'd be too much chance of them being seen."

"We can scout their camp together after dark," she suggested. "If we know in advance what their moves are, it would give us the edge in standing them off."

"I was figuring on going back, but I didn't expect to have anybody with me."

"If you'd rather go alone—"

"No, no. Two sets of eyes and ears are better than one."

"We'd better go back to the village, then," Jessie said. "We'll have to assume the land-grabbers will move tomorrow and make our plans to stop them. It looks like tomorrow's going to be a busy day."

Darkness had settled in when Jessie and Lathrop started back to scout the invaders' camp in the dry riverbed. They looked back now and then, and each time they saw fewer lights in the cabins. Just before they entered the brush and lost sight of the village, the only illumination to be seen had come from the windows of the cabin where the councillors were still talking together, and there was a rectangle of yellow light shed by a lantern glowing inside the council hall.

In the hall Ki had assembled the handful of youths between the ages of fourteen and eighteen who had looked large and strong enough to learn what he had to teach them. Eleven young Ojibways made up the group Ki had chosen, and because time was short he had decided from the outset to teach them the basic moves of only one of the several martial disciplines of which he was a master.

Ki had selected the *bo* as the best weapon for them to learn. It was a simple one, a staff about six feet long, tapered from the center to each end. While a fine craftsman was needed to make a really good *bo,* a usable one could be made quickly, using a straight sapling of wood that was close-grained and hard, but not brittle.

There were good stands of ash and maple trees just beyond the cleared fields, and Ki's pupils all understood the art of shaping wood. Most of the few daylight hours that had remained after he'd chosen his fighters had been spent making weapons. Each of them had made his own *bo* while watching Ki make his, but when Ki first began explaining the weapon's use, Mizuan, Standing Bear's nephew, had appointed himself spokesman for the skeptics among them.

"What good is a stick like this against a rifle?" he asked scornfully. "It would be better if we made bows and arrows."

"A bow is useless when the arrows are gone," Ki said. "A rifle is only a club when the shooter has no more bullets. You must learn to attack when your enemy has no more bullets or is reloading his gun."

"And how will we keep from being shot before he runs

146

out, while he empties his rifle at us?" Mizuan asked.

"We will dress like women and go into the fields to work," Ki told them. "The men will stay close to the houses. There are so few guns that they can hope to do little."

"What if the land-grabbers shoot us as they cross the fields to the village?" one of the young men asked.

"It is a chance we take," Ki admitted. "But if we scatter and fall to the ground as though we are women and afraid, they will be more likely to pass us by than to shoot at us. When they get close enough to the village to start shooting, we will attack them from behind."

"What will keep them from shooting us then?" Mizuan asked.

"They can't shoot if their rifles are empty. We'll have to wait until they stop shooting and reload before we attack." Ki stepped to within a few feet of Mizuan and went on, "Hold your *bo* as you would a rifle that you're reloading. When I run at you, hit me with it."

Mizuan shifted his *bo* to the position Ki described, and Ki rushed at the youth with his own *bo* held in the side-strike attack position. Mizuan swung his staff at Ki's head, but as the arcing blow began, Ki caught Mizuan's *bo* in a counterstrike, stopped the blow, let his *bo* slide free, and reversed it to land a blow on Mizuan's knee. As the Ojibway youth sagged, Ki reversed his *bo* and tapped Mizuan's head.

"If I had used all my strength, I would have cracked your skull," Ki told the lad. "Now do you see?"

Rubbing his head ruefully, Mizuan nodded. "Perhaps I was wrong," he admitted. "I am glad you did not hit me hard. Now show me how this thing is done."

By the time Ki called a halt to the lessons late in the night, the young Ojibways had learned the thrusting and striking *bo* attacks as well as the basic defensive blocks. They were far from expert, but against an unskilled opponent, their blows could be expected to go home.

Because the houses in the village were small, Jessie and Ki were staying in different dwellings; Jessie had been given a room with Standing Bear and his family, while Ki slept in the house of Amik, the council member. Like all the houses except the one where the councillors were meeting, Amik's house was dark. Ki entered quietly, and after his long teaching session he wasted no time going to bed. Shedding his clothes in the dark, he slid under the blanket, and stretched and flexed his muscles to relax them.

As the gentle exercise drained the tension from his body, Ki fell into a light doze, and was dimly aware that deep sleep was only a few moments away. Then the door of his room opened and closed almost at once. Fully awake now, Ki sat up in the bed. His eyes were turned toward the door, but he could see only a vague, formless shape.

A whisper came from the darkness. "Ki?"

Ki recognized the voice. "Shining Water!" he whispered. "What are you doing here? Your father would be very angry if he knew you were in my room!"

"My father is with the other councillors. They will talk until the sun comes up."

"Then your mother might hear you, or miss you from your bed."

"She does not wake easily, and her room is not close."

"This is still no place for you to be. You're far too young to come into my bed."

"No, Ki. You don't know our ways. We Ojibway women do not belong to men, we are free. From the time we are old enough to shed our blood each month, we decide what man we want to sleep with. Only after we are married do we have one man and no other." While she was speaking, Shining Water moved with silent steps to the bed and sat down on it. She went on, "Tonight I choose to sleep with you."

Ki offered her the best excuse he could think of. He said, "I'd be no good to you or any other woman tonight, Shining Water. And tomorrow—"

Work-hardened fingers closed over his lips. Before Ki could remove them and continue, Shining Water was speaking again.

"Tomorrow there will be fighting. I heard my father talking of this thing," she said. "A man needs to be with a woman before he goes to fight, Ki, and I know ways to make a man desire me. Move over, let me lie under the blanket with you."

Ki made a quick decision. He decided that the best way to end Shining Water's attentions was to humor her and let her stay for a moment while he persuaded her to wait for a better time. Resolving to hold himself limp, no matter what efforts Shining Water made to rouse him, Ki shifted his position to make room for her to lie down beside him and felt her warm, smooth skin sliding along his arm, then his hip and thigh, as she worked herself under the blanket.

Chapter 14

Ki did not move as Shining Water began to caress his body with her work-hardened hands. She ran them gently down his chest and across his flat, muscular stomach to his crotch. Her fingers danced for a moment across Ki's pubic arch, but went no lower. He remained motionless. Shining Water lifted her body and slid her torso across Ki's chest, rising enough to let the firm nipples of her full breasts touch his skin with the gentle pressure of a butterfly's soft wings.

She retraced the path her fingers had covered, lowering her body bit by bit as the firm tips moved toward Ki's hips, until they were pressing firmly against his smooth skin. He felt her fingers slide between his thighs and cradle his sex. She lifted his limp shaft and placed it between her breasts, then spanned them with one hand and closed her hand until his member was fully enclosed in the fleshy, warm cushion.

Ki exercised his control to keep himself from swelling and growing hard, but his resolution to discourage Shining Water was beginning to waver. It wavered still more as she crouched lower and brought up her other hand to hold Ki more firmly in the warm crease that encased him, and then began to rotate her shoulders from side to side.

"Do you like this, Ki?" she whispered. When Ki did not reply, she went on, "I'm even warmer inside, and softer.

Don't you want to come into me and feel how I can please you?"

Ki still remained silent and motionless. He was having to use the full force of his will now to keep from responding to Shining Water's caresses. He kept himself soft while she continued her movements for several moments longer. Then, when she felt no stiffness growing in response to her efforts, Shining Water released Ki and knelt beside him. She bent forward and let her tongue dance along his flaccid sex, flicking it from head to base, before she cradled her head on his thigh and closed her lips firmly around his manhood.

For a few moments Ki remained still, but the soft rasping of Shining Water's tongue over the tip of his engulfed member was draining his resolution. He said, "Enough, Shining Water. I gladly give you your victory."

Shining Water did not stop her caresses. Ki let his control go, and when Shining Water felt him growing hard, she drew away and lifted herself to her knees, straddled Ki's hips, and sank down on his rigid shaft.

He lay for a while without moving, his fingers caressing her taut breasts; then, as she began to gasp breathlessly in rhythm with the rocking of her hips, Ki grasped her by the waist and lifted her until he could rise to his knees and lift her with him while still keeping their bond of rigid flesh unbroken.

Shining Water spread her thighs in mute invitation for Ki to drive deep, and he thrust with long, firm strokes as she began to tremble in a rolling, sighing climax. He plunged deeply and with a faster rhythm until her tossing and trembling slackened, and held himself in her, full-length, while her ecstatic sighs died away and she grew still and remained motionless.

Then he started plunging again in slow, even strokes that roused her once more to a frenzy of twisting, heaving gyrations. When he sensed that she was near another climax, Ki let himself go and joined her in a final quivering spasm; then, as her sighs began to slacken, he lowered himself on her lithe body and let himself relax.

"You see?" Shining Water whispered in his ear. "I told you that you would desire me. Rest now, Ki. I will be with you while you sleep, and tomorrow you will fight better for having me in your bed tonight."

Darkness was almost complete when Jessie and Lathrop rode into the underbrush that started beyond the edge of the cultivated fields. They'd had little to say after leaving the council, for the plans they'd been able to make in such a short time were sketchy at best, and both of them were preoccupied, thinking about the moves that had been worked out and trying to find ways to improve them.

A quarter moon provided a ghostly light as they rode into the brush. They talked little, knowing that the intruders might have set out sentries to avoid being surprised in their camp. The dry riverbed where Lathrop surmised that the wagon tracks led was a bare five miles from the village, but in spite of their urgency to reach the invaders' camp, they were forced to move slowly. The area they were crossing had been logged years ago, and now it was a wilderness of small second-growth saplings and brush that hid hundreds of stumps, all that remained of the big trees felled during the long-ago first cutting.

"I don't think the land-grabbers will try to travel through this brush in the dark," Jessie said, regaining her balance in the saddle after her horse had scraped against an old stump and danced away from it. "It'd be bad enough in daylight, when you can see where you're going."

"They'll be crossing it on foot," Lathrop said. "And you

can move faster walking then you can riding in cut-over country like this."

"Why are we riding, then?" Jessie asked. "Let's tether the horses and walk the rest of the way. We'll be able to move more quietly, too."

"Shank's mare it is," the Mountie agreed.

He reined in and Jessie followed suit. They led the horses to the only clear place they saw that would accommodate both animals, and looped their reins around one of the saplings.

"Can we find the horses in this darkness if we need them in a hurry?" Jessie asked.

"My mare's been trained to whinny when I call her," the Mountie replied. "And if we have to leave in a hurry, it'll mean we've been spotted, so the noise won't be important."

Making their way through the tangle of vines and creepers, avoiding the tangle of thin, low-growing branches that whipped at them as they pushed through the dense vegetation, Jessie and Lathrop moved as silently as they could toward the dry riverbed.

After advancing a short distance, they saw the red glow of a fire in front of them, and moved with even greater caution. Before they'd covered a half-dozen yards, the ground underfoot began to slant down and their feet encountered small boulders under the soft carpet of rotting vegetation.

"There's a little clearing along here somewhere," Lathrop said in a half-whisper. "To our left, I think. If we can find it, we can look right down on their camp."

"You know the country," Jessie said. "Lead the way. I'll stay a little bit behind you."

She waited until she could barely hear the soft whispers made by the whipping of low-hanging branches as the Mountie began pushing through the thick growth along the

153

edge of the riverbed, then started following him. They were moving away from the fireglow now, and the darkness soon became impenetrable. Suddenly, from the blackness ahead Jessie heard the whipping of branches, the quick scuffling of feet, and the thudding of flesh on flesh. Ignoring the noise she made, she started running toward the disturbance.

Jessie stopped when she reached Lathrop and the dim figure with whom he was locked in a silent scuffle. The Mountie had evidently attacked his adversary from behind, for he had one arm stretched over the man's shoulder, his palm locked over his mouth and chin. Lathrop was having trouble maintaining his grip; the pair swayed and shuffled as the man struggled to break free.

Drawing her Colt, Jessie swung its barrel hard in a short arc. The barrel and trigger-guard landed with a thud on the man's head. He slumped in the Mountie's arms, and Lathrop lowered his limp form to the ground at his feet.

"Their lookout," he said tersely. "I saw him first."

"Do you suppose there are others?" Jessie asked.

"Maybe. But we don't need to go any farther. This is the clearing I had in mind." Lathrop motioned toward the edge of the riverbed. "About two steps is all we need to take to get a look at their camp."

They moved up cautiously and peered down toward the edge of what had once been a sizable river. The decline at their feet and the level strip at its bottom were covered with boulders that ranged from the size of a man's fist to some that were as big as ponies. Years of scouring from the water flowing over them had removed all traces of soil and left the stones bare.

On the level area at the bottom, a dying fire created a blob of light bright enough for them to make out a number of men huddled in blankets. A lone sentry kept watch by the fire. At the very edge of the lighted area, the rectangular outlines of two wagons were visible.

"Eighteen sleepers," Lathrop said after they'd studied the scene for a moment. "The sentry by the fire makes nineteen, and this one we just took makes twenty. They'll all have rifles, I'd guess, and pistols as well. That's a great big edge over the five or six decent guns the Ojibways have. I don't think Ki and his boys with their sticks can balance this thing in our favor."

"Don't underrate Ki," Jessie said. "You're right, Ben, they are long odds. But when you're in a fix like this, the only thing that's going to tip the scales is strategy, and I think the scheme we set up at the village is going to work out."

"It's too late to change it now," he replied. "All we can do is wait and maybe pray a little bit."

Dawn was just filtering its gray light into the room when a movement of the bed woke Ki with a start. He looked up to see Shining Water standing beside the bed.

She whispered, "You are a strong lover, Ki. I must leave now. Already my mother has gone to the kitchen. We will have another night before you go."

"Of course, Shining Water. If we can."

"There will be breakfast soon. Come to the kitchen when you are ready. You must eat well, for I know there will be much to do today."

Ki's band of young Ojibways was already waiting for him in front of the council house when he got there after breakfast. They were laughing and chatting in their own language, but from their gestures Ki gathered that their joking was centered around the clothes they were wearing.

All of them had on the voluminous dresses that were the

everyday garb of the village's older women. For the most part the dresses were in shades of dark gray or brown, though a few were black. Convincing the youths that they would lose no face by dressing as women to deceive their enemies had been Ki's hardest job the previous day. Getting the women to give up their hard-to-come-by dresses had been almost as difficult.

"Where is your dress, Ki?"Mizuan asked. "Or won't you be with us in the fields?"

"I'll be with you," Ki promised. "But I will not be seen. Today I am going to be one of the hidden warriors that in my land are called *ninja.*"

"How can we not see you if you will be there?" one of the other youths asked.

"You'll see when the time comes," Ki said. "Right now we must go quickly. It's important that we be in place when our enemies arrive."

In a straggling line the group walked to the fields. Ki saw to their placement, trying to arrange them as nearly as he could remember in the kind of pattern he and Jessie had seen the women form on the day when they first came to the village. The group formed a straggling, random line midway between the village and the ragged edge where the cultivated land ended at the edge of the second-growth timber. Ki saw to it when they scattered out between the rows of knee-high wheat that they were always close enough together so that if one of them got into trouble there would be a companion near enough to help him.

When he was sure that the fields looked like they did on any other day while the women were at work, Ki walked slowly to the position he'd chosen for himself. As he walked, he plucked handfuls of thin stems of the green wheat and wove them as though they were thick threads into a long rectangle that would be wide enough to cover him.

Ki knew the loosely woven stems would not hide him, but in his samurai training he'd learned that total cover was not needed to conceal a man stretched flat on the ground. A man could be sufficiently hidden with a loose cover of a color that blended with its surroundings and broke the outline of his body. Even on bare ground it was possible to lie outstretched under such a cover and be overlooked by an enemy.

Glancing back occasionally, as much to keep a check on the Ojibway youths as to make sure he was getting to the position he'd selected after his preliminary look at the terrain, Ki stopped a hundred yards from the end of the field and roughly in its center. He hunkered down and divided his attention between the boys and the weaving that he was now bringing to completion. From time to time he stopped both weaving and watching to stand up and scan the thick second growth and listen for any noise that might be brought him by the shifting breeze.

An hour passed, and then another. At last Ki heard what he'd been waiting for, a distant rustle during a period when the fitful wind had died down. Now he wasted no time. After a final glance at the Ojibway boys, Ki spread the covering on the ground. It blended so well with the sprouting wheat around it that he could not suppress a small smile of satisfaction. Lying down, he pulled the green cover over his body and stretched out flat, almost invisible in the knee-high wheat.

Jessie woke to the soft touch of Sergeant Lathrop's fingers on her cheek. The light was soft in the pre-sunrise dawn. After they'd watched the camp in the dry riverbed for a while when they first arrived, they'd taken turns dozing while the other stood watch. In spite of the broken nature of her sleep, Jessie felt rested as she sat up in response to Lathrop's touch.

"Are they getting ready to move?" she asked.

"Yes. They're all on their feet, chewing jerky. They let the fire die out when the sky started to grow light."

Jessie nodded at the man they'd captured and asked, "Have they missed him yet?"

Their prisoner lay gagged beside a sturdy sapling. One loop of Lathrop's handcuffs was closed around his right wrist, the other around the sapling. They'd gagged him with the Mountie's neckerchief before he'd regained consciousness, and had not dared to try to question him for fear he'd begin shouting. Even a slightly raised voice would have been heard by the men in the riverbed.

Lathrop shook his head in reply to Jessie's question and said, "They're still half asleep. But they're going to start counting heads any minute now, so we'd better decide whether or not we want to risk staying here."

"I suppose there's bound to be a search," Jessie said.

"I think so. And if we try to force him to go with us, he might make enough noise to lead them to us."

"Then let's risk staying where we are," Jessie said. "Our chances of being found are just about the same, whatever we do."

Lathrop nodded and they returned their attention to the men below. They'd brought horses up now and were hitching them to the wagons. Suddenly one of them said, "Hey, where's Rafe got off to? I don't see him noplace."

Another of them grunted and said, "If you ask me, he's done a bunk. He got up during the night, said he couldn't sleep, and was going to walk around a bit. He ain't come back yet, and I don't guess he intended to."

"Now that's a rum go," said the man who'd spoken first.

"It don't matter," the other replied. From his tone and the manner in which the others listened to him, Jessie picked him as the leader. Her guess was confirmed when he went on, "We've got enough to do the job. Rafe just won't get paid when I hand out the pay packets."

"Now that's something I'd like to know about, Nivens," one of the others said. "When do we draw down our money?"

"When the job's finished, just like the other ones. You know better than to ask a fool question like that."

"If we ain't waiting for Rafe, let's get on with it," said the one who'd spoken first. "Sooner we get done, the sooner we get paid, and I've got a fancy gal waiting for me to get back to Winnipeg with money in me pocket."

"All right," the leader said. "You saw yesterday where the wagons are going to wait for you when the job's done. And I guess all of you know what to do."

"How about the ones that wasn't on the last job?" a voice called. "All we know is it's scaring and wrecking."

"All right," the leader replied. "Bust out of the brush and run at the women in the fields. Start shooting as soon as you're out of the brush. Now, mind you, I don't want nobody killed unless you've got to. Aim to hit their legs, unless it's a man with a gun in his hand that you're shooting at."

"That's all it is?" asked the man who'd spoken before. "How do we know there'll be anybody to shoot at?"

"Because the women are always in the fields this time of year, you ninny!" the leader retorted. "Make one quick sweep and run for the wagons. Cleary and Benoit will handle the torches. And you two remember what the chief said. Don't burn down more than three or four houses. He wants the rest standing when he takes the place over."

Jessie and Lathrop watched while the men started up the slope in a straggling line. They were fifty or sixty yards away from the nearest, and the thick brush hid them from any but the most penetrating look. They followed the progress of the attackers by sound, and stood motionless and silent as the rustling of the undergrowth and the scraping of booted feet on the hard ground faded to a faint whisper.

"They won't be looking back," Lathrop told Jessie. "I'd say we can follow them now."

"Yes." Jessie indicated their prisoner. "What are we going to do about him, though?"

"Leave him right where he is. There's not any way we can take him along, and the cuffs ought to keep him where he is until we can come back and get him."

"All right," Jessie said. "I'm ready whenever you are."

They turned and began pushing their way toward the fields. Ahead of them, the noise of the attackers stayed constant until they'd almost reached the end of the second growth woods.

"You stop here, Jessie," Lathrop said. "I'll move a bit farther along so we'll have them in a crossfire. We'd better wait until we've heard their first shots before we move."

"Just as we planned," Jessie said. "Go on, Ben. I'll be there when the time comes."

Lathrop moved off, his course roughly paralleling the line of the dry river's bank. Jessie stood motionless. She'd waited several minutes, each seeming longer than the last, when the first shot rang out from the fields ahead of her. Drawing her Colt, she started working her way through the brush.

Chapter 15

Pushing as fast as she could through the brush, Jessie heard a second shot soon after the first had sounded. She tried to move faster, but the dense growth and hidden stumps slowed her progress. She reached the edge of the second-growth and advanced until she was hidden only by a thin line of the saplings and could look through their low-hanging branches at the fields.

There was still a gap between the advancing attackers and the disguised Ojibway boys, but it was closing fast. The youths were running back and forth in simulated panic, and from a distance their disguises almost deceived her. Then one of the land-grabber gang reached the lad he'd chosen as his quarry and started closing on him, his rifle raised, butt formost, ready to strike. Darting aside, the boy bent down to pick up his *bo*.

He was still in a crouch when the attacker started to bring his rifle butt forward in a smash that would have shattered the boy's skull if it had landed. The Ojibway was ready. He raised the *bo* above his head and deflected the rifle-butt, and as the gun bounced off the *bo*, the youth spun around, bringing the *bo* down to waist-level.

Before the rifleman realized what was happening, the young Ojibway jabbed the *bo* forward in a thrust that caught his assailant on the chin. The impetus of his rush was combined with the force of the thrust. Even at a distance, Jessie heard the crack as the man's jawbone broke. Blood gushed from his mouth and he dropped his rifle and brought his hands up to his chin, a gurgling scream of pain bubbling from his throat as he crumpled to the ground.

Elsewhere on the field, the land-grabbers were receiving the same kind of unpleasant surprise. Though outnumbered almost two to one, the Ojibways were more than holding their own, and Jessie turned her attention to the village. She saw three of the attackers moving along the edge of the field, carrying smoking torches. They were heading for the cluster of small houses, and as they drew closer the Ojibway men who had rifles emerged from their hiding places.

Jessie recognized Amik and Standing Bear, but the other two were strangers. She waited for the defenders to fire, but Standing Bear was the only one who raised his rifle and let off a shot. The slug kicked up a puff of dust behind the torch-carrying runners, but did not slow them down. Even as the threat drew closer, Standing Bear was the only one of the Ojibway men who used his weapon, and his shots were so badly aimed as to be useless.

Suddenly Jessie realized that the Ojibways had been so conditioned by defeat and their long tradition of peaceful coexistence that they could not bring themselves to use their weapons. Even though they held in their hands the rifles that would save their homes from being burned, they were unable to raise the guns and fire. They stood watching the arsonists draw closer, but still refused to try to stop them.

One of the torch-carrying land-grabbers raised his revolver and let off three quick shots at the Ojibway men. Jessie saw Amik stagger backward and grasp his abdomen, and watched while the others turned to help him. Without a rifle, and with the distance between herself and the houses

162

so great, there was nothing Jessie could do. She heard shooting from the field now, and turned her attention back to the youthful defenders.

Two of the young Ojibways had been brought down by the shots Jessie had heard. Seeing their comrades fall, the others suddenly realized that what had seemed a pleasant game was a fight in deadly earnest. They began backing away, and the battle-wise ruffians of the attacking force saw their opportunity. The intensity of their rifle fire increased, and the panicked Ojibway youths began running. They scattered as they moved, and Jessie wondered when Lathrop was going to signal her that the time had come for the two of them to join the fight.

Then for the first time she saw Ki. He rose from the ground, still draped in his green camouflage, and darted toward the nearest attacker. Jessie saw a sparkling in the air as Ki launched a *shuriken*. The star-shaped blade with its razor-edged points sailed through the bright morning air and sliced into the neck of a land-grabber who had his rifle shouldered, aiming at one of the fleeing Ojibway boys.

When he felt the bite of the *shuriken*, the man let his rifle muzzle drop, and the slug kicked up dust from the ground a few yards from his feet. The recoil tore the rifle from his hands, and he began running for the brush, clawing at his shoulder as he ran.

Ki did not break stride, but veered toward another of the young men who was in trouble. Another *shuriken* flashed in its arc and found its target. This time the land-grabber loosed a gargling shriek in the instant before he fell, for the blade had dug into his 'neck and severed his spinal cord.

Hearing the cries of pain from their companions, the other attackers hesitated. From beyond the scene of the fracas, Jessie heard Lathrop's rifle bark, and another of the invaders dropped. Responding to the prearranged signal, Jessie entered the fight. She broke from the brush and started running, to get into pistol range.

Seeing that help had arrived, the Ojibway youths began to slow down, and two of them turned to counterattack. Ki was still in motion, shreds of his improvised green cloak flapping as he ran toward the closest knot of conflict. His weird appearance, as much as the sight of his shining blades describing their deadly arcs, unnerved the land-grabbers. Then Lathrop's rifle barked again. Its slug found another target and the attackers began to flee. They ran in a scattered, disorderly line, slanting across the wheatfield, seeking the shelter of the underbrush that lay beyond it.

Jessie fired twice as the running men streamed past her, but the range was extreme for her Colt. She saw one of her targets stagger and clutch his thigh, but he kept moving. Then she heard the thudding of hoofbeats behind her, and turned to see Lathrop riding up. He led her horse by its reins and tossed them to her when he pulled his mount up beside her.

"I wouldn't have believed it if I hadn't seen it," he said, pushing his wide-brimmed hat back on his head.

"Aren't you going after them?" Jessie asked.

"Yes, of course. But there's no need for me to hurry. If they're running for their wagons, as I suspect they are, there's only one road for them to take. I'll catch up with them soon enough."

"I'll ride with you, if you'd like me to," she offered.

Lathrop shook his head. "No, Jessie. I've put myself out on a limb far enough now, letting you and your friend Ki get into police matters. And the Mountie uniform still commands respect. They won't give me any trouble I can't handle."

"Will you come back when you've taken them to jail?"

"If I can. I've been away from my station too much of

late, and my clerk can't run it on his own forever. You're planning on staying here awhile, then?"

"A day, maybe two. Why? Are you going to come back here and arrest me?"

"Now that'll depend on the instructions I find waiting for me at the station. Let's not borrow trouble, Jessie. There's enough of it to be cleaned up to keep me busy for a month. And speaking of trouble, I'd better be moving on. I'm sure the Ojibways will take care of tidying up their wheatfield."

Jessie watched Lathrop as he rode off, then swung into the saddle of her own horse and kneed it toward Ki. He was standing with the Ojibway youths, who were clustered around one of their fallen comrades. She could see at a glance that Ki was all right, and noticed that his first look had been to assure himself that she too was unhurt.

"How many young men were wounded?" she asked.

"It could be worse. This boy's got a broken thighbone, and there's one other with a bullet in his chest. They've carried him to the village for the women to look after."

"We'd better go there too, Ki. I saw Amik struck by a rifle slug. There may be something we can do to help."

At Amik's house, Shining Water and Aushok, Amik's wife, were standing beside a chair in which the wounded councillor sat. Migizi and Standing Bear were also in the room.

"How badly are you hurt?" Jessie asked Amik.

"I am very sore, but I do not think my wound is bad," he replied. He grimaced as he spoke, but his face soon took on its usual placidity. He went on, "Since you and Ki are here, I know we must have won the fight."

"It was easier than we thought it would be," Jessie replied. "Now that we know you're all right, Ki and I will go see if there's something else we can do to help."

"You have done much," Migizi broke in. "But Amik has more to say." He gestured toward Shining Water and Aushok to indicate that they were to leave the room. When they'd gone, he went on, "We were waiting for you to get here before talking of this thing, Jessie Starbuck. Amik wants to go at once to Treasure River."

"Don't you think it would be better to wait until you've recovered, Amik?" Jessie asked the councillor.

Amik shook his head. "No. What has happened to us today might happen again. We must talk about Treasure River with you, Jessie Starbuck, and we cannot talk until you have seen it."

"Are you sure you're able to travel?" Jessie frowned.

"There is only a short way to go," Amik replied. Turning to the others, he added, "I speak the way my spirit tells me I must. Do not worry about me, I will be all right."

Migizi turned to Standing Bear and asked, "What do you think? We must speak with one tongue on this thing."

"I feel as does Amik. Already we have waited too long to tell Jessie Starbuck why we asked her to come here."

His wrinkled lips pursed, Migizi nodded. "It is what we must do. I feel this too." He faced Jessie. "You will go with us today, then, Jessie Starbuck?"

"Of course, Migizi. I came here to help you any way I can, and even though you've told me there's a place called Treasure River, I still don't know more than its name. So many things have happened that we haven't done more than mention it. If you and Amik and Standing Bear want to go today, Ki and I are ready to go with you."

Migizi frowned. "I am not sure that Ki should go. We have not talked of him, but only of you."

Ki said quickly, "Don't worry about hurting my feelings by asking me to stay here, Migizi. I'll do whatever you decide."

Jessie shook her head. "No, Ki. I think you should go. I don't want to be the only one who knows the secret. If something should happen to me—"

"Let Ki be with us, Migizi," Amik said. "We know we can trust him, as we trusted Alex Starbuck and as we trust Jessie Starbuck. He is one with them."

Standing Bear added quickly, "I say yes too, Migizi."

"Then I will not say no," the old chief answered. "We will go at once. It is not a hard trip, nor is it far, but each hour of daylight is precious. We will go on horseback, for Amik will not be able to walk." He turned to Jessie and went on, "I must tell you now so you will be ready for this thing, Jessie Starbuck. There is water to swim through. Wear what can be dried, and do not bring your gun, for it would be ruined."

A scant half hour later the five rode out from the Ojibway village. Migizi led the way, Standing Bear kept his horse close to Amik's mount behind him, and Jessie and Ki brought up the rear. The old councillor led them directly to the dry riverbed, and along its wooded edge. They rode for perhaps four miles before Migizi reined in.

"We must go on foot from here," he said. He dismounted and took a coil of rope from his saddlehorn. "Come. Follow me."

Migizi started at an angle down the stony slope of the dry riverbed, and the others fell in behind him. The stones were slippery underfoot, and their progress was slow. When they reached the bottom of the slope, Migizi went as far as the center of the flatter area and led the little group along it.

They'd walked in silence for perhaps a quarter of a mile when the smooth, rounded stones of the bed began giving way to shelving layers of granite, and the bed became narrower. A short distance farther on, Jessie saw that the granite layers rose like a dam across the streambed, blocking it completely. She frowned, but said nothing.

Migizi stopped in front of the high-rising wall of granite; it stood perhaps sixty feet above the riverbed. Turning to Standing Bear, he said, "Come. We must open the way."

Followed by Standing Bear, Migizi walked to the corner of the wall, where it stopped at right angles to the steep granite wall that had been the bank of the now-dry stream. He studied the corner for a moment, then nodded and motioned to Standing Bear to come closer.

Pointing to a crack in the face of the wall, he said something in the Ojibway tongue. Standing Bear moved up to the wall and inserted his fingers in the crack. He pulled, but nothing happened. Migizi joined Standing Bear in tugging, but without result. Shaking his head, Migizi turned and gestured to Ki to come to him.

"We will trust you, Ki, as we trust Jessie Starbuck, to keep the secret of Treasure River safe."

"Of course," Ki agreed. "What do you want me to do? Pull at that crack with Standing Bear?"

"Yes," Migizi replied. "I do not have the strength I had when I was younger. And the gate to Treasure River has not been opened for many years."

Ki joined Standing Bear in locking his fingers inside the crack and tugging. They pulled for several moments before there was a creaking and scraping sound, and a section of what had looked to be a solid wall began to move. Able now to get a better grip, the two exerted themselves even more, and the slab moved with slow reluctance until at last it gave way to reveal a slit wide enough for them to squeeze through. Beyond the slit there was only complete blackness.

"Now we must swim," Migizi said. "I will go first, with the rope tied to me. You will have to hold the rope with one hand while you swim. It is only for a short way, though."

Jessie had come prepared for swimming. She took off her boots, blouse, and jeans, and stood wearing only the chemise that she'd decided would be the best undergarment for the occasion. The Ojibways put their clothing beside the swinging granite slab, and wore only loincloths.

Migizi looked around after he'd tied the rope around his waist and said, "Hold tight to the rope. It is very dark in the place we are going."

He stepped through the opening in the wall and vanished in the blackness beyond. Amik, helped by Standing Bear, followed, and Ki gestured for Jessie to go next. She grasped the rope and went through the opening. Two steps inside, the passage curved and the light faded as she followed the curve. She heard a splash ahead, followed by Migizi's voice.

"Remember, do not let go of the rope when you start to swim, and when it goes below the water, breathe deeply before you dive!"

Though Jessie could not be sure, she thought the granite ledge underfoot was sloping downward. The rope grew taut in her hand. She felt the icy chill of water on her feet, then stepped off into the black depths. As she felt the strong tugging of the current, the rope tightened again and she took a deep breath and dived. The rope stayed taut, leading her, and she stroked and kicked through the icy water.

Suddenly the rope slanted upward, pulling her with it. She opened her eyes, expecting to find herself in blackness again, and was surprised to see that she was in a cavern filled with a glow as soft and gray as dawnlight. The water was still black, though the current's pull had subsided. Ahead of her she saw the heads of Migizi and Amik and Standing Bear, and when she looked back, Ki smiled at her.

Migizi was emerging from the water now, walking up a narrow ledge of granite. Soon Amik and Standing Bear joined him, and then Jessie felt the solid rock under her feet. She looked back to see Ki rising from the black water. When she turned ahead again, those in front of her had vanished around a sharp curve in the cavern's solid granite wall. Then Jessie rounded the curve and stopped and stared and gasped in surprise.

She'd entered a huge, dome-shaped chamber, the river now a small stream running alone one side. Through narrow cracks in the dome's upper quadrant, brilliant shafts of sunlight glowed. The sun was not as golden, though, as the glittering gold nuggets that were heaped in head-high piles around the perimeter of the vast underground dome.

It seemed to Jessie that everywhere she looked, she saw the gleam of the precious metal. There were nuggets as big as her fist and others as small as the tip of her little finger. She started to count the heaps, but lost count when she realized she'd tallied one twice. Before she could start again, Migizi moved to her side.

"This is why Alex Starbuck called the dark stream Treasure River," he said. "We do not know where the river flows after it leaves the cavern. Just as it appears from some giant spring below the earth, it vanishes underground beyond this cave."

"And you don't know its source? Or where it surfaces?"

"We know nothing except that it is here. Your father did not know, though he tried to find the place."

"How did Alex find this cave, then, Migizi?"

"This thing he did not tell Kineau, who was our chief councillor when Alex Starbuck was with our people. After Kineau, there was Numae, who got the secret from Kineau and passed it on to me, just as I now pass it to you."

"But do you own the gold, or did Alex?"

"He found the treasure, Jessie Starbuck, but it was on the land he had given us. He gave us his promise that he

170

would not take any gold from the cave without taking an equal amount to give to our tribe, and in return we promised that we would not take any without taking an equal amount to give him. We have not taken any since we made the pact with Alex Starbuck. But now we need to use a small bit of the gold. We sent Standing Bear to bring you here so we could tell you our need, and let you take out your portion."

Jessie stood silent, her eyes traveling over the incredible hoard of riches. She saw Amik leaning on Standing Bear's arm, Ki close behind him, walking slowly around the cavern, looking at the immense treasure. She thought of the miserable poverty in which the Ojibways were living, and knew that Migizi's request was reasonable. Still, having seen the evil effects of rapid overcivilization on other Indian tribes, she hesitated to speak quickly. Migizi stood beside her, waiting with silent patience.

"Let us think about what we shall do, Migizi," she suggested. "We have seen the gold now, you have told me of your agreement with Alex, and I will honor it, of course. But Amik is not strong enough to stay here long. He needs to go back to your village, where his wound can be cared for. Let's talk tonight about the gold."

Migizi nodded. "That will be good. There is no need for great haste. And you are right, Amik must leave quickly." He raised his voice and called to Standing Bear, then added a few words in Ojibway tongue. Standing Bear and Amik turned and started back to where Jessie and Migizi stood. Ki saw them, and turned to follow them.

Amik and Standing Bear had taken only a few steps when Amik grasped at his chest and bent double, his knees buckling as he sagged. Jessie and Migizi hurried to the two. During the few moments that passed before they reached the wounded man, Amik had collapsed in a heap on the stone floor.

171

Standing Bear was kneeling beside him. He looked up at Jessie and Migizi and shook his head. "His heart is barely beating," he said. "I think he is going to die."

Unexpectedly, Amik spoke. "I knew I was going to die. But to learn the secret of Treasure River, I wanted to come with you."

"We will take you home, where you can be cared for," Migizi said. "Come, Amik. You do not want to die."

"No man wants to die, Migizi," Amik replied with a feeble smile. "But all men accept death when they know it is near. No, I do not want to go home. Leave my body here, and I promise you that my spirit will guard the treasure of our people."

"But we can't—" Jessie began.

Standing Bear straightened up. He said, "Amik is dead."

For a few moments they were silent, then Migizi said, "Let it be as Amik asked. We will leave him here. He will have his wish. Perhaps his spirit told him something we do not know."

While Jessie and Ki watched in silence, Migizi and Standing Bear lifted Amik's body and arranged it between two of the heaps of gold. Then, subdued and silent, they left Treasure River and returned to the Ojibway village.

Chapter 16

"There's something that bothers me," Jessie told Migizi and Standing Bear as they sat in the council chamber the following morning. "Any gold we take from the Treasure River cave will have to be exchanged for Canada's money."

"We understand this thing, Jessie Starbuck," Migizi said. "But what is it that worries you about it?"

"When you get money for nuggets, there'll be talk that a new gold field has been found," Jessie explained. "Prospectors will come here, then gamblers and outlaws. Your village won't be safe if that happens."

Standing Bear spoke quickly, before the older councillor could reply. "Jessie Starbuck is right," he said. "It will be like ants rushing to a freshly killed deer. They will dig for gold in our fields, and turn our young girls into whores."

Migizi objected, "But we need the gold for better houses, and a teacher for a school, and many other things."

"You don't need gold," Jessie said. "You need money. And I have more than enough. Let me give you what you need, Migizi."

"We do not ask for gifts, Jessie Starbuck," Migizi said. "We can give you gold from our share of what is in Treasure River."

"Of course. But I'm not asking you to do that."

"We are not beggars, Jessie Starbuck," Migizi said. "Let it be an exchange, as I have said."

"I won't argue, Migizi," Jessie told the old man. "Tell me how much money you need, and I'll see that you get it."

A brief discussion settled the amount, and when it had ended, Jessie stood up. "I must go find Ki now. We have to pack and get ready to go home."

"You are welcome to stay here as long as you wish," Standing Bear offered. "You should rest before you travel again."

"There's something I must settle at once, Standing Bear," Jessie said. "That charge of murder. I don't know how long I'll have to stay in Winnipeg to clear it up."

"Shall Mizuan and I ride back there with you?" Standing Bear asked.

"There's no need for you to do that. Ki and I will take the train. We'll ride Mizuan's horses to the Mounted Police station and borrow horses from Sergeant Lathrop to ride to the railhead, and I'll ask the sergeant to bring Mizuan's horses the next time he comes to the village."

Standing Bear nodded, then asked, "When will you leave?"

"Today, as soon as Ki and I can pack."

"Then we will not say goodbye now," Migizi said. "And we will be sorry to see you go. You are a woman like your father was a man, Jessie Starbuck. We will guard the gold of Treasure River for you, just as we have done for him."

Sunset gold was dyeing the sky when Jessie and Ki reined in their horses at the Deer Horn Mounted Police station. Even before they'd wrapped the reins around the hitch rail, Ben Lathrop came out to greet them. Jessie was immediately aware of a change in the Mountie's manner.

"Jessie! And Ki!" he said, hurrying to hold Jessie's stirrup while she dismounted. He took her hand as she swung to the ground, but did not release it as he asked, "Is there some more trouble at the Ojibway village?"

Jessie shook her head. "No. In fact, things have settled down quite nicely there, so Ki and I are on our way back to the Circle Star."

"I'm glad you stopped here, Jessie," the Mountie said. "I was going to the Ojibway village in the morning to see you."

"I hope it wasn't to serve me with that arrest warrant," Jessie said, smiling. She decided she liked the new Ben Lathrop much better than she had Sergeant Lathrop of the Northwest Mounted Police.

"No. But it was one of my reasons for going. I had a telegraph message from Colonel Ferol that the warrant's been suspended until the Winnipeg office finishes taking another look at Count von Aschenhausen. After the Governor-General got your telegram, he started a new investigation. It seems that after banking hours the count spent his time with some very shady people."

"Well, that's good news," Jessie said. "What was the other reason, Ben?"

Lathrop took a long, cream-colored envelope from the inner breast pocket of his red tunic. "Here's a letter for you from Lord Brereton. I was planning to bring it to the village to give you, since I didn't know when you'd be coming this way again."

"It's probably a repetition of what you heard from your chief in Winnipeg." Jessie tucked the envelope into the pocket of her traveling skirt. "I'll read it after supper."

"Supper, to be sure!" Lathrop exclaimed. "Will you have supper with me in Deer Horn, Jessie? And Ki too, of course."

"Were you planning to eat at Deer Horn?" Jessie asked.

"Well—as a matter of fact, I wasn't," Lathrop replied, adding quickly, "but I know that my clerk's fixing a vegetable supper, and I'm a meat-eater, myself."

Ki had been watching Jessie's reaction to Lathrop's changed manner. He said quickly, "But I have the same taste your clerk does, Sergeant. Would it offend you or your clerk if I took your place here for supper, while you and Jessie had your steaks or roasts in Deer Horn?"

"Why, no," Lathrop replied. "I'm sure Glover will be glad to see a new face across the table from him." He looked at Jessie and went on, "Just as I will, especially one as charming as yours. If you accept my invitation, of course."

"Of course I accept your invitation, Ben. I'd like nothing better."

"Then let me change into my own clothes. If I take you to dinner wearing my uniform, people will think you're a prisoner."

Without the strain that had been imposed earlier on their relationship, when Lathrop had been a policeman and she a suspected murderess, Jessie discovered that the Mountie was a different person. She watched the deft movements of his hands, the laugh-wrinkles that framed his blue eyes when he smiled, and softened his tanned and usually sober face.

They sat late over dinner at a homelike pub in the little provincial village, and when they mounted to ride back to the station, the moon was sailing high in a clear, star-filled sky. The trail followed the rimline of a high bluff from which the lake was visible in the distance as an expansive ripple of moon-silver. Jessie reined in to look across the water, and Lathrop followed her example.

"There's one thing I miss at the Circle Star," she said. "A lake like that one. But even without one, the ranch is still my favorite place in all the world."

"I don't expect you'll be coming back this way again soon," Lathrop said, breaking a silence that had fallen between them.

"Not likely," Jessie replied. "There'll be a lot of mail to be attended to when I get back, and I've been away so much that I haven't given the Circle Star the attention I like to."

"Pity." Lathrop's word just missed being a sigh. "I'd enjoy nothing more than to know you better, Jessie." He added hastily, "Not that I've any romantic illusions. I know the gap between a policeman and a rich young lady like you."

"Why should there be a gap between us, Ben?" Jessie asked.

"Because of what you are and what I am," he answered.

Jessie had anticipated Lathrop's words; she'd heard other men say much the same thing, and had often wondered why they imagined that a woman in her position didn't share the same needs and feelings of those who had less worldly wealth or occupied a different position in society. Long ago, Jessie had decided that rather than go through a life of sterile unfulfillment, she'd always take advantage of fleeting moments such as those that were now passing.

She said, "We've been in an awkward situation, Ben, you a policeman, me accused of being a criminal, but that's all past. Now you're a man—a man I find very attractive, if you want the truth—and I'm a woman."

"Jessie, do you mean what I think you do?" Lathrop asked, his voice showing his disbelief.

"Why don't you find out, Ben?" she challenged.

Lathrop was out of his saddle in an instant, helping Jessie to dismount. He did not release her hand when she stood on the ground, but pulled her into his arms. Jessie turned her face up and invited his kiss. It was a tight-lipped, sterile kiss until she opened her mouth and ran the tip of her tongue

177

along his lips, then she felt his tongue meet hers.

They stood locked in a close embrace until Jessie let her body sag, and in response to her hint the Mountie lowered her to the cool, soft grass. His lips moved across her cheek and traced the line of her jaw, then moved down her throat to the soft, pulsing hollow at its base.

Lathrop's hesitancy told Jessie that this was no time to be coy. With a deft movement of her fingers, she unbuttoned her blouse, and then she pulled his head down until his face was buried in the fragrant hollow between her upthrust breasts. She shivered as she felt the gentle rasping of his chin on her nipples when Lathrop moved to trace the firm mounds with his tongue, and her hand slid down to his crotch and found what she'd been seeking.

Stirring under the weight of her lover's body, Jessie whispered in his ear, "Our clothes are keeping us apart. Let's get out of them, Ben."

They made a lovers' silent game of undressing one another in the soft moonlight, stopping to kiss when the brushing of hands on flesh sent tingling tremors of desire through their bodies. Then they stood naked, face to face, and Jessie stretched out her arms.

"Now, Ben! Take me now!"

Lathrop grabbed Jessie's wrists and pulled her to him. For a second she was suspended in midair, her body erect. She used the moment to spread her thighs and embrace Lathrop with her legs. Her hand snaked down to grasp his rigid shaft, and she guided him to her. She felt him enter her, and tightened the embrace of her legs to pull herself close to him.

"You feel good in me, Ben," she whispered.

"Then this will make you feel even better," he replied.

As he spoke, Lathrop thrust hard and Jessie gasped as he sank full length into the moist recess that was more than ready to receive him. He lurched forward, dropping to his knees, and let his full weight rest on Jessie's soft body. She quivered in response to his deeper penetration, and sighed as he started a quick, hard stroking. His lips were by her ear, murmuring endearments, and Jessie turned her head to seek his mouth, her hips rising to meet his sturdy lunges as he quickened their rhythm.

Jessie found herself approaching her climax. She raised her hips higher and twisted them from side to side in a rolling motion. Her entire body was tingling now. She felt her lover's rhythm falter for a stroke or two, then suddenly he drove faster and with greater force than ever. His gasping breaths were ragged now, almost a series of low sobs.

When she heard his gusty breathing, she knew he was nearing a climax. She was mounting to her own peak now, and gave herself over to the final moments of almost unbearable ecstasy that swept over her in wave after wave until, with a wrenching shudder and a gasping cry, her body was seized by its final responsive spasm as Lathrop exhaled a deep sigh. Then she felt his full weight pressing on her and he lay still.

Slowly the force that had driven them subsided. Lathrop's gasps were further apart, and the shudders that had shaken Jessie's body as she passed her climax were also dying away. She whispered, "Let's just lie here awhile before we start again, Ben. I like to feel your weight on my body."

"And I like to feel your body under mine," he replied. "I don't think we'll have to wait but a few minutes, Jessie. And I'm not going to leave you for a very long time. I want this to be a night we'll both remember."

Leaning back on the dusty, soot-smelling plush seat of the accommodation passenger coach attached to the work train that was taking her and Ki to Winnipeg, Jessie thought of the night just ended, and a smile of remembered satisfaction rippled across her face. She sighed softly and opened her eyes.

Ki, sitting beside her, said, "It is good to be going home, isn't it?"

"Yes. But we'll have to stop in Winnipeg for a day or two, maybe longer, while I try to get that arrest warrant voided."

"Was there anything in the letter you got from Lord Brereton that might help do that?" Ki asked.

Jessie blinked and said, "My goodness, I forgot all about it."

She slipped the envelope from her pocket and opened it. The letter was brief, only a half-dozen handwritten lines expressing the banker's sympathy for her plight and his shock at the revelation of Count von Aschenhausen's duplicity, and offering to help Jessie in getting the arrest warrant voided. She finished reading the letter and was about to hand it to Ki when her memory stirred and she examined the page more closely.

She said, "Ki, please get my portmanteau from the luggage rack. I think I've just stumbled onto something important!"

Opening the small bag in which she carried the daily necessities for a long trip, Jessie took out the scrap of paper that she'd found in the pocket of the count's suit and the one that Lathrop had taken from the body of the man posing as a Mounted Policeman. She compared them with the note from Brereton, then handed them to Ki.

"Tell me if you see the same thing I do," she said.

Ki needed only to glance at the notes and letter before he said, "They're all in Brereton's handwriting, Jessie, and these two notes are obviously written on paper torn from the same kind of paper that he uses for his private correspondence."

"Of course. You can see they've been torn off the bottoms of his engraved notepaper. Lord Brereton was terribly careless, even if he hadn't any reason to think they'd be seen by anybody except the cartel agents he sent them to. I think our first stop in Winnipeg will have to be at Brereton's house."

"You're not going to take the notes to the Mounted Police?"

"No. You know quite well that no police department in the world has ever believed that such an organization as the cartel exists. We'll have to handle this ourselves, just as we do anything in which the cartel's involved."

"Of course," Ki agreed instantly. "And I'm sure you've thought about all the possibilities. Brereton's house servants for instance. A man in his position will certainly have some."

"I'm sure he does. And I'm equally sure that the cartel's bosses wouldn't let a man as important to them as Brereton have any servant who wasn't under their control."

A thin smudge of dawn was just showing in the eastern sky when Jessie and Ki got off the slow-moving work train in Winnipeg and stepped into one of the hacks that was waiting at the curb outside the depot. Jessie gave the cabbie the address that was on Brereton's letterhead, and she and Ki settled into the seat.

Their ride was surprisingly short. The driver pulled up his horse in front of an imposing residence just beyond the city's main business section. Jessie and Ki went up the steps, and while Jessie tugged the brass bell-pull, Ki flattened himself against the wall beside the door.

After a long wait, a burly man opened the door. He'd obviously been awakened by the bell, for he was still blinking his sleep-filled eyes. The neckband of his hard-starched shirt had no collar, and his embroidered livery vest was only half-buttoned. Instantly Jessie pushed her way inside, forcing him to give way. She began talking as soon as she'd entered.

"I must see Lord Brereton at once, this instant!" she said loudly, her voice agitated. "My name is Jessica Starbuck, and I'm sure His Lordship will want to receive me. You can tell him that I have to discuss something very important!"

Only half awake, the man turned to face her, leaving the door half open behind him. He did not see Ki slip stealthily inside and blend into the shadow that darkened the corner of the hallway beside the door.

"I can't disturb His Lordship at this hour!" the servant protested. "It's not even sunrise yet!"

Jessie stamped her foot as a half-hysterical woman might be expected to do. Making her voice even louder and as strident as she could, she repeated, "You must take me to Lord Brereton this minute! He won't be easy on you if he finds out you've turned me away!"

"What did you say your name was?" the man asked, blinking as though her words were just beginning to register.

"Starbuck!" Jessie said, almost shouting now. "Jessica Starbuck! And I demand to see Lord Brereton at once!"

"You have only to turn around to see me, Miss Starbuck," Lord Brereton's voice said in reply. Jessie turned and saw him standing on the stair landing. He was wearing a dressing gown, and a Lancaster repeating pistol dangled from his hand, which was dropped to his side. Brereton went on, "Perhaps you will tell me what brings you here at this inconsiderate hour?"

Jessie replied in her normal voice, "You've been very careless, Lord Brereton. I'm sure your masters in the cartel will discipline you in a very unpleasant way when I arrange for them to learn what you've done."

A frown flashed over Brereton's face, but he regained his composure almost instantly, and his voice was bland when he said, "I can't imagine what you're talking about, my dear lady. You might as well be speaking Greek, which is a language I could never quite fathom, in spite of my tutor's best efforts."

"I don't need to speak any language for you to understand that you're finished," Jessie replied. She took the sheet of letter paper and the two notes from her pocket and held them up. "I'm sure you'll recognize these."

Even in the dim light, Brereton recognized what Jessie was holding. His voice strained, he said, "I'll have those from you at once!" Raising the pistol, he commanded, "Hand them to Scoggins this instant!"

"And do you think that's going to protect you?" Jessie said tauntingly. "Surely you know he reports everything you do!"

His arm extended, Scoggins lurched toward Jessie, reaching for the papers. At the same time, Brereton raised his pistol. Jessie saw Ki's *shuriken* whirring through the air toward the stair landing, and her fine-honed instinct warned her to deal with the closest threat. She stepped aside as the butler grabbed for her, and as she moved, she drew her Colt and fired.

At such close range, a miss was impossible. Scoggins's huge body jerked at the impact of the .38-caliber slug, and took one more step as Jessie whirled to evade him, then crumpled to the floor.

Ki's blade, launched in the instant he saw Brereton start to raise his pistol, slashed into the Englishman's neck. Brereton had his pistol almost leveled before the spurt of blood from his carotid artery drenched his face and dressing gown

183

as it spouted from the deep wound. Like a toppling tree, he fell down the stairs and landed in a huddled heap on the hall floor.

Jessie looked at the two motionless forms for a moment. She glanced at Ki. His face was expressionless.

"I think we can leave without being seen, Ki," Jessie said. "If we walk to the depot slowly, no one will notice us."

Ki gestured toward the bodies. "What about these?"

"Let's leave the cartel a mystery they can puzzle over," Jessie replied. "Perhaps losing their head man in Canada will cripple them enough to keep them from trying anything more for a while. And I want to be on the first train that pulls out of Winnipeg going west. I'm anxious to be in the only place where I can really rest, and I'm looking forward to doing just that as soon as we get back to the Circle Star."